Sex, Murder, Betrayal
Frederick Bruce

Lone Wildcat Books
ISBN: 978-1-7329337-0-5
Sex, Murder, Betrayal/ Frederick Bruce
Paperback & Digital distribution | 2018

This is a work of fiction. The characters, names, incidents, places, and dialogue are products of the author's imagination, and are not to be construed as real.

Dedication

Dedicated to Michael Angelo Panzella,
A man who overcame criticism and obstacles in
pursuing his dreams

Contents

Part One
Scottsdale, Arizona

Chapter One
Telephone Call to Police

At 10:34 p.m. a telephone call was received by the police department in Baytown Beach, California. Baytown Beach is an affluent coastal city in Orange County in Southern California.

The call originated from the Bell Tower Hotel in Scottsdale, Arizona. The receptionist answered, "Hello, Baytown Beach Police Department. May I help you?"

Yes, my name is Carole Benson. I'm a resident of Baytown Beach. But I'm calling from Scottsdale, Arizona where I am attending a seminar. I tried to call my husband at home, but the call went to voicemail. Then I tried to call him on his cell phone but that also went to voicemail. I'm getting concerned because he would always be at home at this time."

"Could he be working late, Ms. Benson?"

"We have our own business in Baytown Beach, but he never works late. Whenever he had work to do, he brought it home," she responded. "I'm worried that he may have fallen at the office or he might have had a medical problem. Could I request a welfare check at the office?"

"What is your husband's name?' the receptionist inquired.

"Charlie. Charles Benson," she answered.

"And what is your home address?" the receptionist further inquired.

"675 Lone Beach Drive in Baytown Beach. "And what is the office address?"

"It's 815 Oak Street in Baytown Beach. It's called Premier Equipment Lease & Rentals."

In response to the receptionist's inquiry, Carole then provided the business, home and cell phone numbers.

"Have you tried to call the office?" asked the receptionist.

"No. I mean, yes, but there was no answer," Carole responded.

"We will dispatch an inquiry and a patrol car will be sent to the home..." Before she was able to complete her response, she was interrupted. "Send them to the office first," Carole directed. "It's just not like him not to be at home and not respond to a telephone call."

"Could he have gone for a late dinner?" asked the receptionist.

"No. That would be unusual for him," she

responded.

"The patrol being sent out will check both locations," assured the receptionist.

"But he's not answering his cell phone," responded Carole.

"Okay, where can we reach you?"

"I'm staying at the Bell Tower Hotel in Scottsdale. Room 1424."

"You'll receive a telephone call following a check of the two locations," stated the receptionist.

"Thank you. I'll be waiting. Have them go to the business first," she repeated.

"Thank you, Ms. Benson."

After the shift commander was apprised of the situation, a police unit was dispatched for what was described as a welfare check. As directed, the first location to be checked was the business address. The dispatched unit with two police officers approached the business on Oak Street.

They immediately observed that interior lights were on in the office. After exiting the police vehicle, they both approached the business unit. One officer approached the door while the second officer remained a safe distance behind. The first officer proceeded to knock at the door.

No answer. After a few minutes, he tried the door. It was unlocked. He then entered the business and called out, "Police. Is anyone here?" No answer.

The two officers proceeded cautiously, walking into a reception area. Again, calling out, "Police. Is anyone here?" Again, no answer.

The two officers unfastened their holsters and each had their hand on their revolvers. They observed a hallway with three open doors and one closed door. One of the offices was lighted, while two were dark.

As the first officer peered into the lighted room, he observed what appeared to be an adult male lying on a leather sofa across from a desk. He then signaled the second officer to look into each of the darkened rooms. One was an office, the second was a conference room. Both were empty. He then cautiously opened the closed door. It was a washroom. It was also   unoccupied. The second officer then signaled to the first officer that the rooms were cleared. He then walked behind the first officer.

The first officer then called out, "Mr. Benson, police officers." No response. He then approached the unresponsive adult male and observed that he was not breathing. He checked his carotid artery and said, "He's dead." A call was then place to the police station. Within a short period of time, several police vehicles arrived. Police tape was utilized and a crime scene was established. The coroner was in route to the location.

A telephone call was placed by the shift commander at the police station to Scottsdale. "Hello, Ms. Benson. A police unit was dispatched to the business that you informed us about. Unfortunately, a deceased male was found at that location."

"It's my husband, isn't it?"

"We can't say. The coroner's office will have somebody there to make a positive identification."

"I'm leaving right now," she said. "I'll be taking the next flight back to Orange County as soon as I can."

After the coroner arrived at the scene, it was determined that the deceased was that of Charles Benson. In a preliminary determination, it appeared that it was a homicide and Mr. Benson died from a broken neck at approximately 5:30 p.m.

.

Part Two
Back in Time

Chapter Two:
Career Beginnings

Most of David Wilson's classmates in the business curriculum at college were looking to enter their careers with large corporations. For long term security and financial rewards, that appeared to be the desired direction for them. Most majored in finance, management or marketing. Entry level salaries appeared to be appealing.

However, David once read in a book by a successful entrepreneur that you will never get rich by working for someone else. Although not true in all situations, it rang true to David, who had very independent leanings. He felt that one had to take risks. If something didn't work out for him, then he could try something else. Nothing was forever. And there were no guarantees.

David's father was employed by an insurance company throughout his working years. Although he did not feel completely satisfied in his career, he made no changes in his employment. He felt that his position with the company gave him a feeling of security. He looked forward to his retirement. Although David understood his father's goals, he could not see himself taking that path in his own lifetime.

David was encouraged by his father to pursue a business education. He was convinced that it would be the best way for David to secure steady employment. Although David was open with his plans to be independent, his father was pleased with the educational direction that David was taking. When David spoke about being an independent businessman, his father would smile and say, "You look at things that way now, but you'll eventually change your thinking."

Thinking that David was young and naive, his father was convinced that David would eventually see the world as he saw it. For that reason, David's father never presented a strong approach to change David's thinking. He just felt that the business environment, as he knew it, would change David's thinking. David's business education would enable him to have the necessary tools when headed in the direction that his father thought would be beneficial for him.

David graduated with a business degree and a major in accounting. His immediate plans were to work for small accounting and bookkeeping businesses. Most of those types of small businesses provided services for other small business. He even offered to be employed on a part time basis with different employers.

David's motivating factor was not the level of wages offered, but instead, was the experience he could obtain in working with a variety of businesses. During tax season he sought positions with tax preparation firms. In his way of thinking, his college education taught him the basics of business. His subsequent training while employed would teach him about business—what you can't get out of a book.

In working with the various business entities, David could see that these owners understood their businesses, but did not always understand what was necessary from an accounting and tax standpoint to keep themselves in business. David's personality and easy going style blended real well in working with the owners of these businesses. He exhibited a strong interest in helping them in their business endeavors.

His genuine attitude and straight forward approach became apparent to the clients. Fortunately for David, he did not appear to the clients like the stereotypical accountants that they had previously dealt with. He had a direct approach that clients felt comfortable dealing with. After all, he was helping them in their livelihood.

What surprised David most was the openness of these clients in discussing personal matters that had nothing to do with their business.

David's employers also saw the strength in David's ability to work with people. More and more, they were having him work with more complex clients. This added to his growth as a business counselor.

Eventually, David desired to leave his parents' household and be on his own. One of David's friends had an older brother who had become an attorney. David had previously met Thomas Finley, but did not know him well. Finley had recently been separated from his wife and moved into his own apartment.

It was brought to David's attention that Tom was looking for a roommate at the apartment. David's friend thought this might be a good fit for his brother and his friend. The two were introduced and the arrangement appeared to be a satisfactory fit for both of them.

Chapter Three
David's Own Business

To some people, it is never the right time to start your own business. David had seen where some people, waiting for the right time, spent their entire career working for others. Leaving the perceived security of an employer can be difficult. But in David's mind, to wait for a time when the economy was more conducive, or to wait for the perfect circumstances to arrive before making his move, may result in him feeling empty and unfulfilled.

David understood these feelings. However, for so long, he had visions of his independence in a business career. Risky? Yes. But, his dreams and desires overrode the risks.

One way to start this business is to open an office, pay for advertising and wait for the telephone to ring. That approach may work if your family can provide you with a sizable financial loan or gift. However, that was not realistic for David.

With some earnings saved from his prior employments, David was able to accumulate enough funds for the start-up expenses. His roommate, Thomas Finley, was beginning a solo legal practice and had a small office that he rented. The office had a small reception area, Tom's office and a small conference room. Tom was also able to employ a part time clerical person who also served as a receptionist.

David's start-up expenses included a telephone at Tom's office that went to voicemail when it was not answered. Business cards were printed, using Tom's office as the location of David's business,

Although that location was shown on David's business cards and his letterheads, the size of Tom's office did not make it feasible for David to see clients on a regular basis at that location. Occasionally, David would use Tom's conference room when it was available. David's approach to grow his business was going to have to be different. His business cards identified him as:

David Wilson
Business Counselor

Many of the business owners to whom David had provided services while employed as an accountant were aware that David was starting his own business. Some of them wanted to switch to David to service their accounting and tax needs. Realistically, these new clients were not sufficient in numbers to enable David to sustain an income flow that would sustain a viable existence in his new venture.

As a new approach, David began what he referred to as cold calling. He would target a business, based on its apparent size, where he thought he could retain and service as a client. He would do this by walking into one of these targeted businesses and ask to speak with the owner. Upon meeting the owner, David would hand the owner his business card and introduce himself as a new business counselor in the area.

That introduction would usually generate questions from the owner as to what a business counselor does. He would then explain that he works with clients to help in their general business needs, with an emphasis on their accounting and taxes. In some situations, he could even provide payroll services.

David was careful not to be too aggressive in his initial impromptu meeting with the owner. In a sense, he was there to create enough intrigue to set up an appointment — not to sell his services. If he was not able to set up a future appointment, he would leave his card and ask them to call him if they ever had any questions.

The approach used by David certainly produced some dead ends. There were times when he entered what appeared to be a small business, only to find out that it was a satellite office for a major multi-national company. Some owners had no interest to talk to anyone offering services. But others were curious enough to engage in a discussion with David. In all situations, he always left his business cards. Even if his services did not fit the situation, people might know someone who might be interested.

As David continued his cold calling on businesses, he became more comfortable in introducing himself to strangers and talking about the services that he provided. As he kept reminding himself, he was not trying to sell his services in the initial meeting. Instead, he was trying to set up a future appointment where he could discuss the needs of a particular business and offer his services to that business.

In one of the more interesting encounters, David

walked into a location where the sign identified the business as *West Coast Motorcycles, Sales & Services.* As he walked through the front door, David noticed two rough looking individuals with long hair and beards.

One of the men from behind the counter called out, "What are you selling?"

David looked at him and immediately responded, "I don't know. What are you buying?"

Both of the men looked at him and broke into laughter. They did not expect that kind of response. *West Coast Motorcycles* subsequently became a client. Sometime later, the one individual who was the owner later told David that when David responded the way that he did, he somehow had a feeling that they would eventually be doing business together.

Depending on the clients' needs, David's services were flexible. Some needed bookkeeping services. Others had an in-house bookkeeper. Most of them needed yearend tax preparation. David would usually set up his services by arranging for at least a monthly visit. In a way, this would insure that he would get paid for his services, and not have to wait for a check in the mail.

Although educated in accounting and taxes, David did not provide all those chores himself. Instead, he contracted with people to handle many of those tasks. For example, for tax preparation, he contracted with various tax preparers. David often referred to these people as tax geeks. They certainly knew their craft, but often were unable to solicit the clients needing their services. David had that ability. The result was a win-win situation for both of them.

Chapter Four
Calling on Premier

David continued his cold calling routine each week in an effort to build his practice. He knew that he had to be disciplined and continue these necessary activities in spite of the significant number of dead-ends.

One day he noticed several small business units on Oak Street in Baytown Beach. That particular section of Oak Street was about two blocks from the downtown area. It was a uniquely quiet street, consisting of several one story business units, surrounded by several taller buildings. It almost appeared to be a hidden street that would generally not be noticed by most people traveling in the area. It could easily be missed.

From the signs, David could see that there was a printing business, a law office and one that was advertising bookkeeping and tax services. Some of the offices had no signage for identification.

Then David noticed a business with a sign identifying itself as:

Premier Equipments
Lease & Rentals

He decided to call on that business and introduce himself.

As he walked into the business, he observed a lady sitting at a desk, facing the front door. "May I be of assistance to you?" she asked in a pleasant tone of voice.

"Yes, my name is David Wilson. Is the owner in?" he inquired.

"Not at this time. May I help you?" she further offered.

Before David had a chance to respond, a lady walked out from one of the offices. To David, she was strikingly attractive, appearing to be in her early thirties. She appeared like a model walking out of an ad. Before David could respond, she said, "My name is Carole. My husband is not in at this time, but is there something I could help you with?"

As David looked at her, he responded, "Oh, my name is David Wilson. I'm a new business counselor in the area and I stopped by to introduce myself, and inform businesses of the services that are offered."

"What type of services do you offer?" she inquired.

"I work with a variety of businesses to counsel

and advise them in matters relating to taxes and accounting. The services provided vary, depending on the needs of each business."

"My husband should be back in about one hour. Would you be able to stop back at about one thirty?'"

"Why, yes. Of course. I'll stop back at one thirty. Oh, and here's my business card," he offered. "I look forward to seeing you, well you and your husband at that time."

David left, hoping that he did not appear too awkward in meeting that beautiful woman. Fortunately, he'll have a couple of hours to gather himself before he returns.

At precisely one thirty, David re-entered Premier Equipment Lease & Rentals. "Oh, hello," was the greeting from the receptionist.

Before David had a chance to respond, Carole walked out from an office and said, "I've got it Clara."

"Oh, hello," David greeted Carole.

With a friendly smile, Carole said, "We can go into the conference room. My husband is there now."

As they walked into the conference room, Carole led the introduction with, "Charlie, this is the gentleman that stopped by earlier that I told you about. And David, this is my husband, Charlie."

"Nice to meet you," each greeted each other almost in unison, and shaking each others' hands. Charlie appeared to be a man in his fifties and one who appeared to be somewhat tired and weary.

"Carole said you were a business counselor."

"Yes I am," responded David.

"And you work with businesses in the areas of tax and accounting," Charlie continued.

"Yes. Depending on the nature of the business, my services vary. It depends on the needs of each business and what I can provide in the way of needed services," David responded.

"Well, this is a unique type of business," Charlie explained. "We purchase equipment and lease or rent the equipment to all types of other businesses. Quite often, it would not be cost effective for them to purchase the equipment needed. They may not need the same equipment for their next project. And even if they did, they usually don't have the funds to make such a purchase."

"I can understand that," David responded, trying to show that he understood and was following the explanation.

"Depending on the length of time needed for the equipment, we either lease or rent. My customers range in size from a one man operation to a large corporate contractor."

"So you actually purchase and own all of the

equipment," David chimed in.

"Yes, and as you can appreciate, we have to keep up with, and be aware of, any new equipment being developed and used on a variety of projects. Obviously, some equipment may be used for twenty years. Other equipment seems to change in design and utility at a more frequent pace. Keeping up with changes in the industry takes much of my time."

"I can understand the need to keep up with that and why one has to be tuned into so many industries," David concurred.

"And of course, we keep all of the equipment in a room in the back of the office," Charlie said with a smile.

"Really?" David responded with a grin.

"Actually, we have a location about a mile from here that houses all of our equipment," Charlie explained.

"I kind of assumed that," David said, smiling.

"So, I'm not sure how we could use your services," responded Charlie.

"I was going to ask about the preparation of your taxes?" David inquired. "Actually, I'm asking who prepares the tax returns?"

"That's a good question. We've had a particular lady prepare our taxes since I started this business," responded Charlie. "She was originally referred to me by a cousin who had an auto repair business. And she also does our accounting. We are satisfied with her work. So, I'm not likely to make a change in that area."

"If you would allow me, I would like to review your tax returns for the last two years," David proposed. "There would be no charge for that service. If I find that all is in order, you haven't lost anything. If there can be some savings, I could inform you of that."

"That won't be necessary," responded Charlie. "If there is nothing else, I thank you for coming in. I need to get started on some projects. But, again, thank you."

Carole, who said nothing during the discussion got up from her chair and said, "I'll walk you to the door David."

David got up from his chair and said, "Well thank you Mr. Benson. I appreciated your time and I find your business very interesting."

He then followed Carole out of the conference room. Before leaving, he looked at Carole and said, "If there is any change, I would like the opportunity to review the tax returns. There are some possibilities in which there might be some tax savings. And, as I mentioned before to Mr. Benson, there is no charge for the review."

"Let me discuss that with Charlie," Carole said.

"I'll be getting back to you, one way or another."

"Thank you Carole." And then David left the office.

As David drove away, he was digesting his discussion with Charlie. Should he have approached it differently? Should it have been presented differently? Well, Carole said she would talk to Charlie. David thought that she might be persuasive when talking to her husband. David was convinced that she must have been a model previously.

Well, enough for the day. David felt worn out. He decided to go home, have a cold beer and watch a game on television. Tomorrow would be another day.

Chapter Five
Manzo Printing & Graphics

The address David used for his business location was the law office used by his roommate, Thomas Finley. This added more legitimacy to the business as opposed to using a post office box. Despite having that address to identify a location, David seldom used Tom's office.

As previously indicated, on various occasions, David sometimes used the conference room when it was available. The telephone in the conference room, as well as the one on the receptionist's desk had buttons for a line that was David's telephone. Incoming calls to David's line that were not answered were routed to his voicemail. When using the conference room, David would make outgoing calls.

Initially, many of the telephone calls made by David were made from the apartment he shared with Tom. Return calls to his listed telephone went to the office, and when not answered, automatically went to his voicemail. Realistically, since he was just getting started, there were not many incoming calls.

David continued his cold calling routine as a primary method to grow his business. One day he was pleasantly surprised when his roommate, Tom Finley, gave him a referral. One of Tom's attorney acquaintances, Ted Harrison, told Tom of an individual having serious tax problems. Tom told Mr. Harrison that he knew an individual who specialized in tax matters. Referrals are an important and an opportune way to build a practice. David understood this and he was very grateful for the referral.

The referral was for a business identified as *Manzo Printing & Graphics.* It was a business owned by an individual named Jack Manzo. As soon as he had an opportunity, David placed a telephone call to the business. "Manzo Printing and Graphics," was the female response after two rings of the telephone. "May I assist you?"

"Yes, my name is David Wilson. I'm calling because I received a referral to contact Jack Manzo," David responded.

"He's busy right now. What is this about?"

"I'm not sure," responded David. "Mr. Manzo had spoken with another individual and asked me to call him."

"Well, okay. Hold on," she said.

David was very careful not to discuss a matter that might be of a sensitive nature, and of course, he would not know who was or who was not privy to the situation. And tax problems would seem to fall into a sensitive area.

"Hello, this is Jack Manzo," came a strong voice, interrupting the silence.

"Yes, Mr. Manzo, my name is David Wilson. I am a business counselor that specializes in tax matters. I had a referral from Mr. Ted Harrison to contact you regarding taxes," as David was trying to set forth his best professional tone and waited for a response.

"Oh, okay," he responded. "I've got a fuckin' tax mess. I was having a drink with a friend of mine about a week ago and he introduced me to an acquaintance of his who joined us. We got to talking about business and the subject of taxes came up."

"Okay," responded David to show that he was listening and following along.

"This guy tells me that he knew someone that had tax problems going back a long ways. Apparently, this guy always filed his taxes, but seldom paid the total amount due. Then the guy goes to an attorney who files a bankruptcy for him and poof, the fuckin' taxes disappeared."

"I see," said David, continuing to listen.

"So I look up some attorneys and then called this guy, Harrison. He instructed me to go to his office

26

and drop off all my paperwork from IRS with his assistant. So I did."

Then there was a pause, and David asked, "What happened after that?"

"I don't know. His assistant called me a few days later and said that Mr. Harrison couldn't help me. They would be mailing back all my paperwork," said Jack Manzo in a frustrated tone. "I was pissed. She then said they would try to refer me to somebody who might help me. I guess you're that someone, right?"

"Well, I would like to get together with you to see if there is something that I can help you with," offered David. "What would be a good time to get together?"

"I don't know," Jack answered, and then paused. "Could you stop by at five?"

"Yes, I'll be there," David responded, and proceeded to get the address of the business.

At precisely five o'clock, David walked through the front door of *Manzo Printing & Graphics*. He was greeted by a mature woman wearing an industrial apron.

"Hello, I'm David Wilson," he said to the woman.

"Jack did say that someone would be here at five. Well, you're certainly not late. Have a seat," she offered. "He'll be up in a minute." With that, she then walked to the back of the shop.

27

As she promised, a short time later, a man came from the back of the shop. "Hi, I'm Jack Manzo," he said as he greeted Jack with a handshake.

"Hello, I'm David Wilson. Do we have a place where we can talk?" he asked.

"Not really. Hold on," and he walked toward the back of the shop. He could be heard saying, "Helen, can you finish up those letterheads. Okay, just leave them on the counter when they're done. If I'm not back, just lock up before you leave."

Jack walked up to the front. "Let's go across the street. We can talk there."

"The two of them walked across the street and entered an establishment called *Sam's Bar and Grill.* "This will be more comfortable for us. No interruptions," Jack explained. The two of them sat down at a table in the back of the bar. "Just for the record, I named myself after my business. I shortened my name to Manzo. My real name was too long. Nobody could spell it or pronounce it. After a while I realized that it made so much more sense to change my real name to the business name. Hence, I became Jack Manzo."

"What was your real name?" David inquired.

"Don't ask," Manzo responded with a grin.

"On the telephone, you said you had a big tax problem," David said to start the discussion.

"Yep. The IRS is breathing down my neck,"

answered Jack as a beer was brought to the table for him. "What are you drinking?"

"I'll just have a coke," answered David.

"The beer is a routine activity each time I enter this joint. It's my usual door opener when I come in here," explained Jack as he pulled out some papers from a folder.

David reviewed the accumulation of letters from the Internal Revenue Service. It didn't take him long to realize the problem, and how far back it extended. He was then ready to explain the situation to Jack Manzo, with respect to his business, his obligations and his dilemma.

"After you contacted the attorney, Ted Harrison, he presumed that you were going to bring him problems consisting of your personal income taxes. Under the rules and guidelines, those types of taxes can be discharged by filing bankruptcy. In other words, if they were filed and were old enough, you would no longer have the obligation to pay them," David explained in detail.

"Right. Well, they're old enough," Jack added.

"Unfortunately, these are not your personal taxes. These are your business withholding taxes. These are taxes that were withheld from the wages of your employees. You were the custodian of these taxes and you had an obligation to withhold them. Then the amount that was withheld was required to be sent to the IRS. In effect, they are trust funds and cannot be discharged by filing a bankruptcy.

"Ouch. So what do I do now?" inquired Jack.

"I recommend that I get a power of attorney from you to enable me to discuss the situation with the IRS," David offered. "Then I will try to work out a payment arrangement with the IRS that is workable and allow you to continue in business. I could deal with them on your behalf."

"That makes sense to me," concurred Jack. "I'm tired of dealing with those bastards."

"I think it would be best to handle the matter that way," David further explained.

"Let me tell you what happened a month ago," Jack said. "I was waiting for a sizable check from one of my accounts. Those IRS bastards confiscated the entire check from my customer. I called the agent handling the account. I told him that it was a good thing that we were not in the same room at that time."

"What did he say?" asked David.

"Nothing. There was silence from their end. I just hung up the phone," added Jack.

The power of attorney was prepared. Jack signed it and paid David a retainer fee to start his representation of Jack and *Manzo Printing & Graphics.*

"Let me get going on this'" said David. "I'll be

getting back to you. The two men shook hands and David left.

David submitted the Power of Attorney to the Internal Revenue Service and negotiated an installment agreement that Jack Manzo felt he could live with. It was not going to be easy for Manzo, but he didn't have much of an alternative.

As he did with all of his clients, David would make appointments with his clients and see them on a regular basis. With Jack Manzo, the appointments were usually set after the regular workday at five or five thirty. And the routine was to walk across the street and meet at *Sam's Bar and Grill.* As they sat down at the table, Jack said he had a story to tell David.

"Last month," he started, "my monthly payment was a little late."

"What happened?" asked David.

"Well, it was due on a Tuesday, and I received a call from the agent on Thursday. I told him I would be in his office before the close of business on Friday," Jack went on.

"And you brought it in to them, right?" responded David.

"Not exactly. I sound like a commercial I recently heard," Jack answered with a grin. "We had an emergency printing project here. So what I did was put the payment in an envelope and had one of my

31

employees take it to the post office and send it by priority mail."

"Well, then they should have received it, right," David responded, going along with the story he was hearing.

"Well yes, but there was a wrinkle," Jack countered. "You see, on Monday morning, we had a visit here from two IRS agents. They had their guns drawn and pointed down at their sides."

"Are you serious?" David questioned.

"Yes," answered Jack. "They identified themselves as IRS agents and said, 'We're here for the check.' I was almost in shock. My employees were frozen in stunned silence."

"You're serious," said David.

"I told them that I sent the payment by priority mail on Friday. I asked them to call their office. They agreed to do so," continued Jack. "After making the call, they told me that the check did arrive at their office.

Then they thanked me and started to leave. I said, 'wait a minute. Why the guns?' Then they told me that it was necessary, because I threatened them with my last contact on the telephone."

"Really?" asked David.

"Yes. After they had confiscated my money from my customer, I said something about them being lucky that they were not in the same room with me

32

at that time. I guess they considered that to be a threat."

"Well, I can see what they're thinking," commented David.

After discussing some other business matters, Jack said, "Oh, I need to tell you something else. My wife and I split up."

"I'm sorry to hear that," David said.

"Well, realistically, we were in a bland marriage," Jack went on. "Our adult daughters are on their own and we seemed to have nothing going between us."

"How did your wife respond to the split," asked David.

"She said okay. I guess my reading of the situation was accurate," lamented Jack.

David just sat there listening, as he does with many of his clients.

Jack then sounded as though he was going to change the subject. "But since then I met this other woman. She seems to be good for me. I don't know if you noticed, but my hair has a different style. I'm dressing better. She's a take charge woman and that's what she's done. Maybe I needed that in my life."

David continued to listen, smiling and nodding at what appeared to be the appropriate times. Being ready to end their meeting, they set a time for their next scheduled appointment. David left, while Jack stayed for some more refreshments.

At their next scheduled appointment, approximately two months later, they again walked over to *Sam's Bar and Grill.* They reviewed the business operations at *Manzo Printing & Graphics.* Jack assured David that his installment agreement with the IRS was continuing on a timely basis. Each month, he found the time to hand carry the payment to the IRS office and get a receipt.

After completing the discussions regarding Jack's business, Jack then said, "Oh, by the way, I need to update you on my situation."

David knew that a major part of his business counseling practice was listening to his clients talk about their non-business life and activities. A business counselor was one that business clients trusted and confided in with much of their business dealings that are not for open discussion with others. As such, the business counselor was the one person that they could talk to about several matters.

Jack, continuing to update David on recent events, expressed his current frustration by saying, "This woman that I told you about before is now driving me crazy. She's a real take charge person. And at the time, I thought that it might be something that I needed in my life. Well, she's gone way beyond what I may have thought I needed."

"Well, you're not obligated to her. I don't think. Unless there's something I'm not aware of," David queried.

"No, not really," answered Jack. "But, here's what happened recently. My wife and I are separated at this time, you know."

"You did tell me that," answered David.

"One day, recently, we had to get together to sign some insurance papers. Since we had to meet and get the papers signed, I offered to buy her dinner after I closed the shop one evening. Well, we went to a nice restaurant and we had some wine with our dinner. Things seemed so different with her. Actually, it was feeling like our early years together. Well, one thing led to another, and before we knew it, we were checking into a motel."

David listened. He didn't say a word. He just smiled as Jack went on talking.

"Now, here's the crazy part— as if what I just said was not crazy enough. After we left the restaurant, we left in my wife's car. I left mine in the restaurant lot. Why, you say? Because, I did not want to take a chance and have my girlfriend see my car parked at a nearby motel."

"Now what," asked David. "I mean, what's going to happen now?"

"I don't know," answered Jack. "I really don't." Later the two men concluded their meeting and set a date and time for their next appointment.

Chapter Six

Contact from Premier

After having breakfast one morning, David called to check his voicemail messages. The first two were solicitation calls—one offering a free website and the other advertising for an upcoming seminar. The next one immediately caught his attention.

"Hello David. This is Carole Benson from Premier Equipment. Could you give me a call at your earliest convenience," she said. "I'd like to ask you a question."

Wasting no time, David picked up his cell phone and called Premier Equipment. After two rings, he was greeted with, "Premier Equipment, Clara speaking, May I help you?"

"Hello Clara. This is David Wilson. I'm returning a call from Carole Benson."

"One moment please," she responded and he was put on hold.

"Hello David. This is Carole," she said in a soft comforting voice.

"Hi Carole. I had a message to call you."

"Yes. After you left the office, my husband Charlie and I were discussing your offer about reviewing our tax returns. I know that Charlie did not show much interest. But we discussed it that day, and then again a few days later," she continued. "I explained to him that we had nothing to lose. If you found everything in order, nothing changes. On the other hand, if you find something that can help us, then we gain something from that point forward."

"That's exactly right," David agreed, realizing that Carole had used his pitch to persuade her husband to change his mind.

The two of them set up an appointment to meet at Premier's office to pick up copies of the tax returns for the past two years. David felt ecstatic for a few reasons. He could be getting a new client. What he said must have gotten through to them — at least to Carole, enough so that she was able to convince her husband. And, although he played it down to himself, he was going to see Carole again. But he told himself that this was strictly business.

After David picked up the tax returns from Premier Equipment, he started to review them as soon as it was practical, considering his other responsibilities to other clients. He had an idea about what he wanted to look at initially.

Premier Equipment made many large purchases

of equipment. Most of it was financed. A few years earlier, the tax laws were changed with respect to businesses. To stimulate the economy, two provisions were added. The first was identified as bonus depreciation. This allowed businesses to write off a major portion of the depreciation in the early years, instead of using a straight line method to calculate the depreciation write-off over the life of the equipment. By increasing the amount of depreciation in the early years, the income is correspondingly reduced. As a result, the tax rate was then applied to a lower base. Therefore, taxes were reduced.

The second tax law change was even more significant. It was called an investment tax credit. More importantly, it was tied to the purchase of equipment. A tax credit was calculated. This was significant because it was applied to the taxes that were calculated. In effect the credit derived reduced the taxes dollar for dollar.

The lady that prepared the tax returns for Premier Equipment was essentially an old family friend that had provided services to their family for many years. David presumed that, although she worked hard and was accurate, she did not understand the changes in the tax law that affected businesses.

Sure enough, in his review, David found that the

bonus depreciation and the investment tax credit had never been applied. He wrote up his analysis and his proposal to amend the tax returns. By law, he could only go back two years. He was ready to meet with Premier Equipment.

David called Premier Equipment and set up an appointment to discuss his findings. He made sure that both Charlie and Carole would be present. Upon his arrival, the three of them met in the conference room.

David first explained the tax law changes from a few years earlier. He covered the purpose for the change — that they were implemented to stimulate business. He showed where Premier Equipment was the perfect business to take advantage of the changes in the law. However, Premier Equipment failed to take advantage of these tax benefits. With the number of equipment purchases made by Premier, the result was substantial.

David then suggested that the returns for the last two years be amended to take advantage of the bonus depreciation and the investment tax credit. David assured Charlie that these amendments would not trigger an audit by IRS. It wouldn't because these were obviously oversights that were made on the return. The adjustments were not changes to income or expenses, which could likely trigger an audit.

Charles Benson was pleased and very impressed with David's knowledge and expertise. He was developing a confidence in David's ability as a business counselor. He gave his blessings to David to amend the returns. "What about going back beyond the two years?" he asked.

"No," David answered. "The tax law limits one to go back only two years to amend their tax returns."

"That's too bad," responded Charlie

David glanced at Carole. She seemed to be beaming. After all, she came out a winner. She persuaded Charlie to bring David back. And he came through for them with great benefits.

Through the process, from the initial meeting to the end result, David had a feeling that Carole liked having him around. Nothing was really said, but he had those thoughts. Maybe it was the way she smiled at him. Either way, it was something he was feeling.

As agreed, David would get the amendments prepared. In addition, Charlie asked him if he might take a closer look to review their business operations. If he were to be out of the office, then Carole can assist him on whatever records or documents he may need.

Chapter Seven
Referral from Premier

T he following week, after David had met with Premier Equipment, he received a telephone call from Charles Benson, the owner of Premier. Mr. Benson was calling David to refer him to a potentially new client. The referral was for McCarthy Building & Excavation.

McCarthy was owned and operated by John McCarthy. Although large in scope, John McCarthy had not incorporated his business. Instead, he continued to operate the business as a sole proprietor. Premier Equipment had some significant equipment leases with McCarthy, and had been doing business with him for several years. Apparently, John McCarthy had had some kind of falling out with his accountant and needed help in accounting and taxes.

David called on John McCarthy to discuss David's services. It did not take long for them to agree to work together. John McCarthy paid David a sizable retainer to start the process.

The biggest priority for McCarthy was the

preparation of the tax return for John McCarthy, which included his business, McCarthy Building & Excavation. John McCarthy had already filed an extension for his tax return, and the new due date was a month away. As David worked up some preliminary figures, he realized that there would be a substantial amount of taxes due. And unfortunately, John McCarthy had paid a very small amount compared to the calculated tax liability.

David had some preliminary discussions with McCarthy about this dilemma. McCarthy's response to David was to hold off on completing the tax return until McCarthy was able to take a closer look at the numbers. Subsequently, McCarthy provided David with a series of transactions that made significant changes in the preliminary figures that David was previously working with.

David was concerned. The return had not yet been prepared. However, changes resulting from McCarthy's data would result in a much reduced tax liability. On one hand, David did not have any desire to prepare a tax return that was not accurate. On the other hand, this client would generate significant fees to David's practice. Then again, maybe McCarthy was accurate with his input.

David decided to discuss the situation with Thomas Finley to seek his legal advice regarding the situation. Tom told David that there might be some concerns about the situation. Between the two of them, they thought it was possible that the books and records of the business were in disarray. That may have been why McCarthy had a falling out with his previous accountant. It is also possible that the original records were accurate and McCarthy was avoiding the payment of taxes that would be due.

David informed Tom that this was a good client for his business and he would hate to lose the business based on speculation that something was improper. David could be wrong in that assumption.

David introduced Tom to McCarthy and the three of them sat down to discuss a proposed direction and solution to the situation. McCarthy could retain Thomas Finley as his attorney. In turn, Thomas Finley would hire David Wilson to have the tax return prepared.

The tax return would be prepared by David, based on the records provided to him. If, at a later date, Tom explained to McCarthy, it was determined that the records were incorrect, then an amended tax return could be prepared and filed.

The attorney client privilege would protect David because he would be employed by Tom, an attorney. David, being employed by Tom, an attorney, could never be called to testify to anything in relation to the accounting records and tax returns. This was agreeable to McCarthy, and they moved forward with the agreement and understanding.

After Thomas was retained by John McCarthy as

his attorney, the extended tax return was timely filed, based on the records and transactions provided by McCarthy himself. Subsequently, after spending several months reviewing the accounting records, David found that McCarthy's records used to file the tax return were erroneous. A corrected set of records would result in a substantial amount of taxes due, including interest and penalties. David explained that to McCarthy.

McCarthy said he understood and that he would be agreeable to filing an amended tax return. He further informed David that the timing was right for him because he had just completed several projects and had a healthy increase in his cash flow. Previously when the extended tax return was filed, he lacked the necessary funds to pay the taxes. Now he had the ability to pay them.

No audit notice was ever received from the IRS. David continued to provide accounting and income tax services to John McCarthy and McCarthy Building & Excavation.

Chapter Eight
Counseling Premier

Following the amendment of the income tax returns for Premier Equipment for the prior two years, David started to review the tax preparation for the next return to be filed by Premier. This was what he and Charles had agreed upon to make sure the next return was accurate and all credits would be received. He began coming to Premier's office on a weekly basis. He would set himself up in the conference room for his review.

He was generally greeted by the receptionist, Clara. After a brief discussion with Charlie, David would continue with his review. As indicated previously, David's usual procedure on his client visits was to initially sit down and talk with an owner. It was during these discussions that various issues regarding the business would arise.

The client would usually update David as to what was happening in his business. Sometimes the conversation would center on the growth or the lack of growth of business. David would comment on various methods that may help the client. This was essentially the role of a business counselor. From the perspective of the client, the business counselor was used as a sounding board for the operation of a particular business.

Usually after David would obtain the necessary input for a tax return or other report that had to be filed, he would take the data with him. When the tax return or other documents were completed, David would return to the client to review the documents or reports before the client would sign and have them ready for filing.

This was the routine when David had the income tax returns amended for Premier Equipment. However, Charles Benson was very impressed with the work done on the amended income tax returns and substantial refunds coming to Premier. For that reason, Charles wanted to expand David's role in his services to Premier. As a result, David was engaged to review all of Premier's accounting and tax procedures. This required David to spend more time at Premier.

In effect David was regularly setting up shop at Premier in their conference room. He would obtain the records as needed, review them and return them. This process continued, enabling him to do a thorough review of the operations. It would have been cumbersome and not practical for him to take the documents with him. Also, in that way, no documents left Premier's facility.

Usually, the records and documents were retrieved by Carole. Charlie was often out of the office seeing his customers and engaging in other business activities, Carole, being knowledgeable about the business operations, could usually answer all the questions that David would generate in his analyses.

On one particular occasion, after David had arrived, Clara mentioned that Charlie was out of the office. Shortly after, Carole came out of her office to greet David, "Charlie won't be here this afternoon. He had a meeting with one of the clients and was going on to a dinner meeting at one of the social clubs. I can assist you in whatever you might need."

"Oh, okay," responded David. "I was going to take a look at the accounts receivables ledger today."

"I'll get that for you," said Carole as she smiled at David.

Carole was always smiling at David. He was thinking that this was probably her usual style with people. However, he did notice that her smile and her presence was more abbreviated when Charlie was in the office. When Charlie was not in the presence of the two of them, it appeared to David that Carole was becoming somewhat of a flirt. That was okay with David. She was nice to look at. However, he was careful not to appear as though he was reciprocating with any flirtatious responses. After all, this was business. And Premier was a good client. They had also referred other clients to him. And there may be more referrals, based on his service and the results that he could achieve.

David started working with the accounts receivable ledger and made some notes to discuss with Charlie. After a couple of hours, he heard Carole say, "Good night Clara. I'll see you in the morning."

Carole then appeared at the door of the conference room. "After Clara left, I locked the front door," she told David. "It gets dark early and I don't feel comfortable with the front door unlocked."

"That's understandable," responded David. "And I'm sure Charlie understands that when he returns to the office."

"Actually, as I had said, after Charlie's meeting, he was going directly to a dinner meeting tonight. Usually they meet in the bar and have a few drinks before the actual dinner at the organization," Carole explained. "He'll just go straight home after the dinner. I'll just meet him at home."

"I won't be too much longer today on this review. I'll walk you out when I finish," offered David. "As you said, it gets dark early this time of year.

"Carole gave David a smile and said "Thanks."

About ten minutes later, Carole appeared at the conference room door and asked, "How's it going?"

"Just about ready to wrap up for the day," he answered as he closed the books.

Carole then said, "I'll be back in a minute."

A couple of minutes later Carole appeared at the door of the conference room and said, "I know you've been looking for a while. And I'm sure you've been waiting to see these."

Having said that, Carole pulled open her blouse and exposed her bare breasts. David just stared. Without thinking, he just reacted with, "They're beautiful," as his face reddened.

Carole then sat down on a chair and said, "Come over here, close to me."

Again, with little thought process, David walked over to Carole and faced her as she sat in the chair. With deliberate movements, she reached out and unbuckled David's belt, unzipped his trousers and slid his shorts down.

David just stood there saying nothing. He was hoping that his knees would not collapse. He was thinking how beautiful she looked.

Carole reached out and completely covered him with both hands. She then leaned forward and enveloped him with her mouth.

There was no stopping her as David started to

breathe heavier. After a few moments he realized that it was going to happen. He just stood there as the words that flowed from his mouth were, "Oh, Carole."

She was done.

He moved back and sat on the chair nearest to him.

"As she sat back, she smiled and said, "I wanted to make you feel good."

As his breathing began to recover to a normal pace, David just looked back at her and smiled, not knowing if he should say anything.

Carole got up and left the conference room. David could hear that she went into the washroom. He then put himself back in order.

After a short time Carole came back to the conference room. "I really need to get going," she said to David.

"Yes," David answered. "I'll walk you to your car."

As they left, Carole locked up and the two of them walked out from the back door of the office. As promised, David walked Carole to her car. She smiled and said, "I'll see you next time," She then drove off in her car.

David walked to his car. He got in and sat for a moment. He told himself, "I think I'm in love with that beautiful woman." He then left for home.

Chapter Nine
Accounting & Tax Practice

David continued to build his practice. He still did his cold calling to obtain new client prospects. Realistically, less time was being spent on cold calling, and for a good reason. He was increasing his clientele by referrals from other clients as well as referrals from other professionals, as they became aware of David and the services that he provided.

Another factor limiting his time for cold calling was the time he was spending on his accounting and tax work with new and existing clients. This was good because he was receiving fees for his services. It was certainly what he was striving for when he started his practice.

As was his routine, David made regular appointments with his regular clients, depending on the nature of his services were to each particular client. As such, David was scheduled for a return appointment with Premier Equipment Lease & Rentals. It had been two weeks since his last visit there when he and Carole were together in the conference room.

There was no question in David's mind that this appointment was going to be somewhat awkward. He hadn't seen or spoken with Carole since his last visit to Premier. And he would be seeing, and working with her husband, Charlie. He was determined to keep his business visit professional.

As usual, he was greeted by the receptionist, Clara. "Hello David, how are you?"

"Just fine," he answered. "How are you doing Clara?"

"Hanging in there," she answered. "Mr. Benson is expecting you."

Just then, Charlie walked out of his office. "Hi David. How are you doing?" he greeted David.

"Good. I had left you some notes regarding the accounts receivables," he stated.

"I did see them. We can discuss that, but I wanted to ask your opinion on some equipment I was reviewing," Charlie said.

"Okay," agreed David.

"Carole, can you bring in those quotes on the construction equipment?" he called out.

Carole walked in with some folders. "Oh, hello David," she extended a greeting with a smile. "How are you?"

"Good," he smiled back at her. She then sat down in the other chair across from Charlie with the folders.

Just then, Ciara called out to Charlie and told him that his auto mechanic was in the lobby to see him.

"Hang on a second," Charlie said. "I need to let him know about my car." With that, Charlie left his office.

Carole then showed David the information on the construction equipment. She started to discuss the quotes on the equipment that were presented to Charlie. There was no hint of anything unusual from his last visit.

When Charlie returned, the three of them continued to discuss the construction equipment. After about an hour or so, they concluded their discussion.

David needed to leave to go to another appointment with another client. Charlie then asked if they could meet the following week to further discuss the accounts receivables that David was working on. David said he would come back and finish his analysis and then he could be ready to discuss it as well as his proposals on the entire project. Charlie said that would work out well. David then left and went to his next appointment.

As he drove off, he was thinking about Carole. Her demeanor was pretty much business as usual. Granted, Charlie was there. However, there were certainly times when they were alone. But there was no indication from Carole that David was anything more than a business counselor to Premier Equipment.

David started thinking about his last visit. Maybe Carole was feeling some desires that she harbored and was exhibiting them with David. That's quite possible. After doing some more thinking about it, she may have thought that the situation that could develop was not good for her marriage or for their business.

David could understand that. From his standpoint, Premier Equipment was a good client and had referred other clients to him. He also needed to be professional. Well, in that case, he would file that incident in his mind under the category of "nothing ever happened." David was not the type to boast of any conquests. The nature of his practice was such that he kept confidences about clients to himself. That was professional and appropriate. End of story.

During the following week David went to Premier Equipment to keep his scheduled appointment. He was going to complete his analysis on the accounts receivable. He would then present his analysis and recommendations to Charlie. Upon his arrival, he was greeted by Carole.

"Hi David, How are you?" she greeted him.

"Hi Carole Clara must be at lunch," he surmised.

"No. She called in sick," she explained. "Nothing serious. I think it was a cold."

"Well that's good."

""I put the accounts receivables and the folders in the conference room for you," she told him.

"Is Charlie here?" he asked.

"No. Believe it or not, he had a golf tournament he did not calendar before he set the appointment with you," she answered. "I'll be in my office if you need anything."

As she walked away, David thought that she really looked nice. She was wearing a black sweater and a black skirt. It wasn't a mini skirt, but it was a short skirt. She was being her usual professional self. Nothing needed to be said about anything else, other than business.

David worked on the project to completion. He made his analysis and would be ready to discuss his recommendations with Charlie during their next meeting. He picked up the files and carried them to Carole's office. She was sitting at her desk when he got to the doorway.

"I've completed the project. I didn't know where you keep these," he remarked.

"You can just leave them in the corner of the conference room on one of the chairs," she responded. "Here, I'll show you."

David followed her into the conference room.

"Just put them in that corner on that chair," she directed.

He followed her directions.

"Is that it for today for you?" she inquired.

"Yes, no other appointments today," he answered.

Just then she walked toward David and smiled at him.

In a voice just above a whisper, she said, "I'm not wearing any panties."

"Really?" came his response, almost inaudible.

"I thought I'd make it easy for you," she offered.

With a deliberate response, David lifted her skirt, in a gesture to confirm her veracity. She was serious.

Without any further hesitation, David slowly moved Carole to the large chair and proceeded to further acquaint himself with this desirable woman.

Later the two of them walked out of the office together and left in their separate cars.

Chapter Ten
David and Carole

Activities between David and Carole became more frequent. David continued to set appointments with Charlie. They met to discuss the review and analysis of the business activities of Premier Equipment.

During their meetings, David was careful not to show any signs of his attraction to Carole. However, he did realize that he was becoming more obsessed with her. He was even having feelings of jealously, knowing that she would go home to the same house with Charlie. Still he had to be careful not to display any signs of his feelings for Carole while at the offices of Premier Equipment. Despite his efforts, he could not get Carole out of his mind or his consciousness.

There were occasions when he was able to talk to Carole in a private setting. They had even made arrangements to meet outside of the office. The routine was to have Carole leave her car in a shopping center parking lot. The two of them would drive in David's car to a small motel in an obscure part of the county.

On one occasion, after an hour or so at the motel, Carole began to talk about Premier's business.

"I realize that Charlie started the business, but things have changed," she opened.

"What do you mean," asked David.

"I've worked very hard to learn and understand the business. And now I am a major part of the business," she went on. "I've been a good partner in Premier's operations."

"I can understand and appreciate that," commented David.

"Charlie has changed. He seems to be more concerned with his golfing and his dinner meetings with his friends," she continued.

"Of course I'm not there on a regular basis, but I hear what you are saying," added David.

"What I'm really saying is that if something ever happened to Charlie, I could run the business," she put forth.

"If something happened?" queried David.

"Yes, I mean if Charlie had a heart attack , or became laid up in some manner, the business would not fall apart," she explained. "I could run it."

"I'm sure you could," David assured her.

"I'm saying that because I have to think of the future, you know, my future," she continued. "Charlie does not take care of himself. He never goes to the doctor. With his weight, diet and smoking, he's a health risk."

"I didn't realize that," said David.

"And, of course, if something were to happen, I know that you would be there to give me guidance and support," she added with a smile, and reached out for David's hand.

"Of course," assured David, as he responded by holding her hand.

A short time later, the two of them left the motel. David drove Carole to her car in the shopping center parking lot. The two cars departed the shopping center and went their separate ways.

As David drove away, he thought about the conversation with Carole. She had never talked like that before. He was not sure what initiated that discussion. Was she getting frustrated with the business— with her husband, or with her marriage in general? He didn't know.

Was he getting too involved? This was a little troubling to him.

Chapter Eleven
Carole's Fitness Program

David commented to Carole that she had a great figure. She told David that she maintains a regular physical regimen. She works with a fitness trainer at a local spa.

As time went on, David realized that he was becoming more and more obsessed with Carole. He would think about her every day. He was finding excuses to drive by Premier Equipment. He continued to find reasons to analyze various aspects of the business. He would tell himself that just seeing Carole would satisfy him each day.

His obsession was taking more time out of his days and weeks. He continued to drive by Premier more frequently. If he saw Charlie's car, he would often avoid stopping. However, if the car were not seen, he would stop by with some excuse.

On one particular occasion, he stopped by. As he entered the business, he saw the receptionist, Clara. "Is Charlie in," he would ask, knowing the answer.

"No, he had an appointment today," answered Clara. "Did he have an appointment with you?"

"No, I was just in the area and I was going to check out something with him," David fabricated. "Carole's out also?"

"She'll be back in an hour or so. She went to the gym," Clara informed him.

"Okay, I'll check back with them later. Nothing that urgent," he told Clara. "I'll catch them next time"

David then left, but he still wanted to see Carole. He decided to drive around the area to check out some of the local fitness locations. He was looking to see if he could see Carole's car. It seemed that he drove around about a half hour before he spotted Carole's car.

David decided to park his car and go into the fitness location. From his car, he grabbed a gym bag that he carried around containing various incidentals. As he entered, he briskly walked past the attendant as if he was a member. She asked if she could help him, but he said he had to drop off something for a friend.

As he looked around, he could see Carole at the far end of the center. She was working with a trainer. The trainer looked like a body builder. David started feeling uncomfortable seeing them working together. Maybe this was all on a professional basis, but he still felt uncomfortable.

David decided to leave the fitness center. He

walked out and got into his car. The car was started and he positioned it so that he could see when Carole was leaving and walking to her car.

Then Carole walked out of the spa. David got out of his car and walked over to see her. She was surprised and said, "Oh hi. This is a surprise."

"Yes, I was in the area and I happened to see your car. I miss seeing you," he told her.

"I miss you too," Carole responded.

"Can we get something to eat?" David asked.

"Oh, I can't now, " said Carole.

"How about coffee?" David pressed.

"I just can't. I'm late. I have to meet Charlie for a dinner meeting," she explained.

"I miss you," David repeated himself.

"I'll call you and leave you a message in the next day or so to let you know when it would be a good time, Carole responded. "You know I have to be careful."

"Yes, I know," answered David. "I'll be looking forward to your call. As soon as you can, I hope."

"I will. For sure," she promised.

David watched as Carole got into her car, smiled, and drove away.

David waited a few days, but Carole did not call or leave a message for him. He was starting to feel ignored. The delay was concerning him. David was thinking about Carole constantly and continually. It was interfering with his business activities.

A few days later, he drove past Premier Equipment. As he drove by, he saw Charlie's car, but not Carole's car. He decided to drive by the fitness center. Sure enough, he saw Carole's car in the parking area. Instead, of going into the center, he decided to wait until Carole came out.

After about twenty minutes, Carole came out of the center. She was not alone. With her was the fitness instructor that he saw her training with in his prior visit. They walked over to Carole's car. They had a conversation that seemed to last a long time. Realistically, it was probably about eight or ten minutes.

Carole then got into her car. The fitness trainer walked over to another car and got in. He drove off. David waited until Carole started her car and drove away. David decided to follow her, being very careful not to be observed. There was no stopping him. He was compelled to follow through with his curiosity.

He followed her as she entered a strip mall and stopped at a liquor store. He parked his car several spaces away, but close enough where he could still see the doorway of the liquor store.

After about ten minutes, Carole emerged from the store with a small bag. It appeared to be a bottle of wine, as the neck of the bottle could be seen from the top. She got into her car and drove away.

David continued to follow Carole's car. He was feeling some stress, anticipating what might be happening. This was his girl. His love interest. How could something like this happen?

To David's surprise, Carole drove to Premier Equipment. After stopping the car, she got out of the car and carried the bag containing the bottle of wine. She then entered the office. As David observed, Charlie's car was still in the parking area.

This was somewhat of a relief to David. But at the same time, she was spending time with Charlie. That also was bothering him. He decided to drive away and go home.

David continued to do work for Premier Equipment. Specifically, he was analyzing their accounting procedures and handling their tax matters. However, realistically, he was reaching a point of completion of his reviews. He would have less activities at Premier.

Charlie was reluctant to change from his present tax preparer. Changes based on David's analyses were implemented. However, Charlie did not want to terminate the services of the woman who was preparing his tax returns for years.

To David, less frequent visits to Premier became disheartening to him. He was seeing less of Carole. His contacts with her were by cell phone and with less frequency If it were not a good time for her to talk, she just didn't accept the call. Other times, they did talk, but she was not going to be able to see him.

David found himself thinking about Carole continually. At times, he would drive by the business. If he saw her car, he would just continue on his way. However, if he did not see her car, he would immediately drive to the gym where she did her exercising. David was not being honest with himself. Although he denied it to himself, he felt some discomfort, knowing that Carole was working out with her handsome and muscular trainer.

As he drove by, if her car was not in the parking lot at the gym, he would just move on and try to do his work. If, however, he saw her car, he would wait until she came out of the building. When she did, he got out of his car to greet her. He would then talk with her. Often, she needed to get back to the business.

There were times when they would set up a time when they would make arrangements to go to a motel. After one such occasion, David told Carole, "I'm not seeing enough of you."

"I am married, you know," she responded. "With my husband and the business, I just don't have the kind of time that you think I might have."

"I understand, but I would just like to see you more," he said.

"You'll just have to be patient for now," she said, hoping to console him at that moment.

"Okay," responded David.

As he thought about what was said after they parted, David was not really sure what she meant, advising him to be patient for now. However, he never pursued her for an explanation.

David just waited for the next time that he could see Carole and be with her. He would try to be patient. He tried not to let his emotions get the best of him. He also had a business to pursue.

Part Three
Murder Investigation

Chapter Twelve
Investigative Team

Investigation of a murder was not a routine chapter within the pages of the Baytown Beach Police Department logs. As can be recalled, there had been only one murder in the past twenty years. It involved a very elderly couple where the wife was suffering from a terminal illness. The couple had apparently agreed to a murder suicide pact.

Only part of the plot played out. After the husband had used a pistol to murder his wife, he changed his mind and decided not to go through with the second part of the agreement. For that moment, he thought that suicide was not the answer for him.

When the police arrived on the scene, the husband confessed to the crime. The investigation took very little time. This crime was the only recorded entry in the listing of murders in the Baytown Beach Police Department records.

For the last several years, Patrick O'Brien held the title of Detective for the Baytown Beach Police

Department. He had been employed by Baytown Beach for over thirty years. Originally, he was in uniform and eventually left the streets to become a plain clothes detective.

Most of his activities were involved with drug crimes and burglaries. As implied, a murder investigation was a new arena for O'Brien and the entire police force. Ironically, this new venture was coming at a time when O'Brien was closing in on a planned retirement. Although assistance was being offered from neighboring police departments, O'Brien declined to accept any involvement from any other agencies. This decision may have had its source in the pride of this detective or he may have thought of it as his final chapter in his law enforcement career.

The Chief of Police for Baytown Beach deferred to O'Brien as to whether assistance would be needed. However, there was another factor in the Chief's decision to go along with O'Brien's preferred approach. O'Brien did, in fact, have some assistance. Three months earlier, Baytown Beach hired Steve Harrington on a part time basis.

Steve Harrington was previously employed by Scotland Yard in London, England. Before he retired from Scotland Yard, he had vacationed for several years in the Mediterranean area on the French coast. He loved it. Then a cousin living in the United States told him that he should take a look at southern California. The climate was similar to that of the Mediterranean and there are other benefits that he might like.

Eventually Harrington had taken his cousin's advice and took a trip to southern California. He very much liked Orange County. While in Orange County, he stopped by and introduced himself to the Baytown Beach Police Department. In addition to being initially charmed by his English accent, everyone became very impressed with this visitor. After he explained his plans following his retirement from Scotland Yard, it was not long before Baytown Beach was agreeable to his employment on a part time basis.

The Chief of Police thought that this might be an interesting combination for the department. Although Patrick O'Brien was born in the United States, he was very Irish. He spent many years in police work. He was now going to be paired with an Englishman from Scotland Yard—an interesting duo, according to the chief.

Although their working time was initially very formal for the first few weeks, it warmed up when, one day after work, Steve Harrington suggested that he and Patrick O'Brien go down to the local pub for a pint. To Harrington, this was an opportunity for the two of them to really get to know each other. It worked.

Chapter Thirteen
Crime Scene

Following the coroner's determination that the death of Charles Benson was a homicide, the two detectives were called on to do the investigation. Their first order of business was to examine the crime scene. They drove to the location of Premier Equipment. As they entered the office, they were met by two uniformed officers at the location.

"Hello, I'm Detective O'Brien and this is Detective Harrington," said O'Brien as each displayed their badges to the uniformed officers. "Where is the body?"

One of the uniformed officers led the two detectives into the office where the body of Charles Benson was located. The coroner was still performing his routine examinations. The parties introduced themselves.

O'Brien and Harrington observed that the body was lying face down on the leather sofa. No blood was seen.

"Cause of death?" O'Brien inquired.

"Broken neck," responded the coroner.

"Approached from the back by the perpetrator. Appears very efficient."

"I've never been here before, but it appears that very little was disturbed in this office," observed O'Brien.

"No. It does not appear that there was any kind of struggle," added Harrington. "Could have been somebody that the deceased knew. Or just met as a customer or prospective customer."

"He appears to be in his fifties," said O'Brien.

Just then, one of the uniformed officers appeared at the doorway of the office. "We have a visitor. A lady who says she is employed here," he informed the group.

"We'll talk to her," said O'Brien, walking out of the office and heading to the reception area, with Harrington close behind.

"Hello, I'm Detective O'Brien and this is Detective Harrington. I understand that you are employed here."

"Oh, hello," said a visibly shaken lady. "My name is Clara. I work here as a clerk and receptionist. Mr. Benson was my boss. His wife Carole called last night and told me of the terrible news. She advised me to stay home, but I just couldn't stay away."

"I'm very sorry for your loss. This must have been a shock," said O'Brien.

"Yes. I still can't believe it," she responded,

wiping away some tears with her sleeve.

"I'm sorry, but since you are here, I'd like to ask you some questions," continued O'Brien, attempting to speak in a soft comforting voice.

"Okay, I understand," responded Clara.

"Were you working yesterday?"

"Yes. I left at noon," she said.

"Who was here at that time?" asked O'Brien.

"Mr. Benson," she answered as she stopped, holding back some tears, but continued to wipe her eyes.

"I'm sorry. I'll be as brief as I can," O'Brien continued in his calm tone.

"Was Mr. Benson expecting anybody that afternoon?"

"No, not that I know of," she responded.

"Does he, I mean, did he usually work late? What I'm asking is, did he work late, like after hours, after five o'clock?" O'Brien went on.

"No, never," said Clara. "He and Mrs. Benson usually walked out at the same time that I did."

"Mrs. Benson, I assume is his wife, right?"

"Yes, that's right," confirmed Clara.

"Was Mrs. Benson here yesterday?'

"No, she was in Arizona at a seminar," said Clara.

"Did Mrs. Benson say she would be here today?"

"No. I'm not sure if or when she will be in. As I said she called me late last night with the terrible news. She asked me not to come in this morning. Then she did ask me if I knew the schedule. She said if someone had been scheduled, I should call them and cancel any appointment that might have been scheduled," Clara explained.

"Well thank you Clara," O'Brien said. "That's all for now. We'll call, or stop back later. Again, thank you, and sorry for your loss. Oh, by the way, was anybody scheduled to see Mr. Benson this morning?"

"Let me check," she said as she opened a desk drawer and picked up what appeared to be an appointment book. "It looks like he was going to meet Alex Johnson for lunch. I'd better call Mr. Johnson," she answered, and then held her head down, trying to hide her face.

"Thank you Clara. Again, sorry for your bad news. I know this must be difficult, but we will be here for a little while. Don't take this the wrong way, but it's probably best that you not remain here while we continue the investigation," said O'Brien.

"I understand," responded Clara.

The detectives left her alone to make her telephone calls, and then observed her leaving the office.

They continued to work with the coroner to learn as much as they could regarding the time of death as well as observing any additional details in that particular office and the other rooms in the entire business unit.

Chapter Fourteen
Investigation

After a few days, a call was placed to Premier Equipment by Detective O'Brien in an attempt to contact Mrs. Benson. O'Brien was careful not to intrude on any funeral arrangements and wanted to give Carolyn Benson some bereavement time following the murder. They were able to reach her by telephone and set up a time to meet at Premier Equipment to ask her some questions as part of their investigation.

The two detectives, O'Brien and Harrington, arrived about fifteen minutes before their scheduled time. "Hello. I believe it was Clara, if my memory serves me correctly," greeted Detective O'Brien.

"Yes, that's right," Clara answered. "Mrs. Benson should be here any minute. She went to the gym this morning, but she was expecting you. I'm sure she'll be here shortly."

"Oh, that's okay," said O'Brien. "Actually, we're here a little early. I guess we wanted to make sure we were not going to be tardy'" explained O'Brien with a smile.

"Can I offer you some coffee or a cold drink?"

"Oh no, we're fine. I did want to ask you a question, Clara. Did Mr. Benson see many visitors here at the office?" inquired O'Brien.

"Not really. It seems as though most of his business was conducted by telephone, fax or email," answered Clara.

"But Premier leased and rented equipment, if I understand the nature of the business," O'Brien further inquired. "Where was the equipment?"

"Actually, it's at a different location. The construction customers would go directly to that location and pick up the equipment that they leased or rented. Quite often, equipment would be rented for a long period of time," she further explained.

"I see. So you did not see many customers at this office during the work day? But you routinely spoke with them by telephone'" continued O'Brien.

"That's true. In fact, there are many customers that I have never seen," explained Clara. "I probably saw Mr. Wilson more than I saw most of our customers."

"Mr. Wilson?"

"Yes, David Wilson. Mr. Wilson is a business counselor that has been working with Premier Equipment for many months. He has been reviewing the business operations and the taxes for

Premier Equipment," explained Clara.

"And he had been working with Mr. Benson?"

"Yes. But it seems that most of his time at the office had been spent with Mrs. Benson," responded Clara. "Oh, I didn't mean to say it that way. That makes it sound a little awkward. I didn't mean it that way. It's just that Mrs. Benson was always at the office, while Mr. Benson was out seeing clients or at some function."

O'Brien and Harrington didn't say anything, but just smiled and nodded, seemingly to understand the explanation.

Just then, Carolyn Benson walked into the office, "I'm sorry, I'm running a little late.

"Not at all. We're early," clarified O'Brien.

"If you can just give me a minute or so?" she said as she walked toward her office.

"Of course," responded O'Brien and Harrington almost in unison.

After about five or six minutes, Carolyn appeared at her office doorway and invited the detectives into her office, "I can see you now."

O'Brien and Harrington got up off their chairs in the reception area and walked toward the doorway of Carolyn's office. O'Brien opened the discussion saying, "Let us express our condolences on the loss of your husband."

"Thank you. It has been a difficult few days,"

Carolyn responded as she sat down in her chair. "Please have a seat."

Harrington spoke up, "We understand that this has to be difficult, but we want to do all that we can to resolve this terrible crime."

"You're British," Carolyn exclaimed.

"Yes I am," responded Harrington.

"I have always wanted to take a trip to England," she said.

"And I was persuaded to come here," said Harrington, smiling. "I was told that the climate was very similar to the Mediterranean, where I had gone on holiday for many years. And I was told that there are so many additional benefits to living here as opposed to living on the Mediterranean. So here I am."

"That's interesting," added Carole.

"We did need to ask you a few questions about your husband," said O'Brien, jumping into the conversation. "I assume that you worked along with your husband in the business."

"Yes, we worked in the business together since we were married eight years ago. I pretty much learned on the job," she explained.

"Do you have plans at this time to sell, or otherwise, leave the business?" O'Brien inquired.

"No. I plan to continue operating the business on a regular basis. I think my husband would have wanted me to do that," she responded. "Over the years I learned the operation of the business, and I am confident that I can continue to keep it going."

Harrington stepped into the conversation, saying, "Before you arrived, we were asking Clara about regular visitors to your business, and more recently, well within the past week, what visitors or customers came here."

"Well, we don't have too many that come in here," responded Carolyn. "Lease or rental arrangements are made and equipment is picked up at a yard that we have near here."

"That's what Clara was saying," answered Harrington. "So there wasn't a long list of visitors."

"Apparently, David Wilson was the most frequent visitor for the last several months," O'Brien stated.

With a sudden change in her smiling appearance, Carole stated, "He's not a customer. He's an advisor that has been helping us with accounting and tax matters."

"I understand that he actually worked more with you than he did with Mr. Benson," O'Brien added.

"Mr. Benson hired him to look into our taxes and our accounting procedures," she explained. "Mr. Benson was very pleased with his advice and his assistance on improving those areas of the business. Since I was always in the office while my husband was meeting with clients outside the office, I would be here to assist in providing any records needed. This was a very good account for David, I mean Mr. Wilson."

"We'd like to talk with Mr. Wilson," said O'Brien. "Do you know how we can reach him?"

"Yes, I can get you one of his business cards," offered Carole.

"Thank you Mrs. Benson. We won't take up any more of your time for now," said O'Brien. "And again, we're sorry for your loss. We'll do our best to resolve this crime."

"Thank you. And here is Mr. Wilson's business card and here is one of my business cards," offered Carole. "Thank you. I feel that you will do your best to solve this terrible crime."

O'Brien and Harrington left the offices of Premier Equipment and drove away.

As they drove away, the detectives discussed the interview they just concluded with Mrs. Benson. O'Brien led off with, "That was very interesting."

"In what way?" questioned Harrington.

"First of all, that was a good looking lady with a great figure," explained O'Brien. "Her husband must have been some stud to maintain a woman like that."

"Or a very rich one," responded Harrington, in an attempt to make a stab at explaining what some women find attractive in a man.

"Well that could be," responded O'Brien, seeming to be agreeable to Harrington's thoughts.

Harrington then offered, "Did you notice the change in her demeanor when the subject of David Wilson was brought up? I found that quite interesting."

"How so?" questioned O'Brien.

"Well, putting that scenario together with Clara's comment that this Wilson guy spent quite a bit of time with Mrs. Benson," Harrington opined.

"Yes, and she immediately said that her husband was very pleased with Wilson's work," O'Brien recalled.

"That's true," said Harrington. "But maybe Benson wasn't aware of all the activities that Wilson involved himself in," Harrington offered with raised eyebrows.

"I don't know. But it does seem that Wilson knew a lot about the business. He may know something about Benson's business and the people that he dealt with," O'Brien started to consider. "We should pay a visit to see this Wilson guy. He could provide some interesting information."

Chapter Fifteen
David Wilson Interview

A call was placed to David Wilson by Detective Patrick O'Brien. As with most calls to David, the call went to David's voicemail. The message asked David to return the call to Detective Patrick O'Brien regarding the death of his client, Charles Benson from Premier Equipment.

David returned the call to Detective Patrick O'Brien.

"Detective O'Brien here."

"Hello, this is David Wilson returning your call."

"Thank you for returning my call so promptly," responded O'Brien. "Mr. Wilson, I'm part of the team investigating the death of Charles Benson. My understanding is that he was a client of yours."

"Yes he was," confirmed David.

"Mr. Wilson, as you can appreciate, I did not know Charles Benson," explained O'Brien. "Because of that I am making an effort to sit down and talk to the people who knew him. If I could sit down with you and ask you some questions, it would be beneficial in our investigation."

"I can understand that," responded David.

"When would be a good time to get together at your office for a meeting between us?" asked O'Brien. "I don't want this to be an inconvenience. Let me know when it can be worked into your schedule."

"Let me check the schedule and see when the conference room would be available. Let me put you on hold Detective O'Brien."

About a minute later David came back on the line, "Would this Thursday at two be okay?"

"That would work," confirmed O'Brien. "Mrs. Benson gave me your business card. Is that address still good?"

"Yes," confirmed David and the meeting was set.

Detectives O'Brien and Harrington arrived at the Law Office of Thomas Finley five minutes before two on Thursday. As they entered, they were greeted by a receptionist.

"Hello, I'm Detective O'Brien and this is Detective Harrington. We were scheduled to meet David Wilson here at two."

"Yes, he's been expecting you. Let me buzz him," she said. "David, your two o'clock appointment is in the lobby"

David walked out of the conference room to

meet the detectives. "Hello, I'm David Wilson," as he held out his hand.

"I'm Detective O'Brien and this is Detective Harrington," as they held out their hands in response to David.

"Let's meet in the conference room," offered David, as the two detectives followed him into the conference room. The three of them were seated and engaged in some small talk about the weather and some of the current events in the news.

David explained that he occasionally uses Thomas Finley's law office, but usually meets his clients at the client's place of business. He explained that his initial contacts with prospective clients are the result of cold calling on a prospective client. He explained that he first met Charles Benson at Premier Equipment by calling on the business in that manner.

"So you would always meet Charles Benson at Premier Equipment? He never came here to meet you?" asked O'Brien.

"Yes, it was always at Premier. He had never been here. The way I conduct my practice, there was no need for him to come here," explained David. "I explain to my clients and prospective clients that it was a convenience to them and they never have to take time coming to my office."

"I see where that would be a good feature for

your services and a convenience to your clients," agreed O'Brien.

"As I explained, I meet my clients at their business locations. Premier was no different. We get into discussions about a client's business. Some work is done there, but most often, if there is a need for more extensive work, I would take the work with me. I then work on a project, usually here in the conference room, and then take it back to the clients in a follow up appointment," explained David.

"It is our understanding that you did do some projects at Premier Equipment in their conference room. Apparently, you worked with Mrs. Benson on some of the projects. Is that accurate?" asked O'Brien.

"Well, if Charles was not there, I would work independently in the conference room. If I needed any particular documents, Carole, I mean Mrs. Benson, would provide me with them. We didn't really work together. Did she tell you that we worked together?" David questioned.

"No she didn't," responded O'Brien.

It was becoming a little obvious that David was becoming a little uncomfortable. His face became flushed and he continued to clear his throat.

After a moment, O'Brien opened with, "Let me ask you, Mr. Wilson, did Mr. Benson ever express to you that he was having any problems with any particular customers? You know, money, financial arrangements, or anything that might be a problem or a potential problem?"

"Not that I can recall," responded David.

Harrington then inserted himself into the discussion with, "You see, it's a bit confusing to us. Charles Benson, by all accounts, seemed to be a well liked chap. We haven't come across anyone that had a bad thing to say about him. He golfed, partied at the bar with several different and assorted buddies, and has been described as quite a jolly fellow."

"As I got to know him, I would have to agree with that assessment of him," answered David.

"Was he like that when you first called on him?" asked O'Brien.

"Not at first. He seemed a little reserved, and a little skeptical regarding the services that I offered. But then Carole, again I mean Mrs. Benson, explained to him that my services could be a benefit to Premier," explained David, suddenly hoping that his explanation was not misleading to the detectives.

"Well, as we indicated to you, this is somewhat baffling to us'" said O'Brien. "But we certainly thank you for your time."

The two detectives then left the conference room

and left the office.

As they drove away, the detectives glanced at each other. "That was interesting," O'Brien opened.

"How do you mean that?" asked Harrington.

"Well, for a while it seemed pretty routine, but then I felt a shift in gears when the subject of Mrs. Benson entered the conversation."

"I hear what you're saying," said Harrington, following along. "I thought that I detected a big change in his demeanor."

"Call me crazy, but I was feeling similar vibes when we were with Mrs. Benson and the name of David Wilson worked its way into the conversation," O'Brien continued.

"You're not suggesting that any rumpy pumpy was going on between them, are you?" questioned Harrington.

"What?"

"I'm saying, well, how do you say it here, any shenanigans going on between them?" Harrington responded with an attempt to offer some clarification.

"Well, I don't know, but we move in a direction guided by our gut. You know, a gut feeling about something," O'Brien tried to explain.

"You think we need to have a further discussion with Mrs. Benson?" asked Harrington.

"I'd say that's our next move," O'Brien continued.

After thinking for a while about the interview with the detectives, David decided that he would call Carole. When calling, he told her that he had just met with the detectives. He explained that he was getting an uncomfortable feeling following some of their questions. Carole asked why he felt that way. And then, almost interrupting herself, she said she would like to discuss his concerns.

"I can stop by if you're available," he said.

"No, let's not meet here," she answered. "Why don't we meet for coffee. How about the *Coffee & Bakery* on Fourteenth Street. I can meet you there in fifteen minutes."

"Okay, I'll see you there," responded David.

David drove to the *Coffee & Bakery* and waited in his car. As soon as he saw Carole drive up, he got out of his car and walked over to where she was parking. It had been a few weeks since he had seen Carole. To David, she looked as good as ever.

As he leaned in to give Carole a hug, she stepped back and reached her hand out to shake his. "Not here," she said. The two of them walked into the coffee shop.

Carole walked over to a table in the back of the coffee shop. David followed her and asked, "Small black?"

"Yes," she answered.

David went to the counter and ordered two small

black coffees. Being a routine order, he waited until it was served and then carried the cups to their table.

Carole looked at David and said, "I don't want you to think that I'm paranoid, but we need to be careful. You know, since Charlie's death was so recent."

"That's what I wanted to talk to you about," said David. "During the discussion with the detectives, I was getting a little uncomfortable."

"Why?"

"They were implying that we were working together. I guess it was the way they were talking and the way they were looking at me," explained David.

"Well, we did work together," confirmed Carole.

"I know. Maybe I'm reading too much into the situation. I don't know," David offered.

Carole looked back at David. "I missed you."

"I missed you too," David responded.

"Do we really need this coffee?" Carole asked.

"Not really," answered David.

"Then take me somewhere."

With that directive, David and Carole got up from their chairs and walked toward the door. As they exited the coffee shop, Carole walked over to David's car. He responded by opening the door and she got in.

Without saying another word, David drove to the motel that had been the location of their prior rendezvous. After parking, he got out of the car and walked into the office. Within a few minutes, he returned, got in the car and drove to a location in the back of the motel complex. The two of them got out of the car and entered the motel unit.

David was feeling that this was a woman that he just could not resist. She was beautiful. And he convinced himself that her body appeared to have been perfectly sculptured. He did miss her.

At the conclusion of their activity, nothing was said. Then, after a while, Carole turned to David and said, "I want to thank you for everything."

David looked at her and said, "What do you mean?"

Carole just looked back at David and smiled. She then got up, picked up her clothes and went into the washroom to get dressed.

The two of them left the motel and drove back to the coffee shop where Carole got out and said, "I'll keep in touch, David, but we have to be careful for a while." She then got into her car and drove away.

David drove away, thinking about what happened during the last two hours. As he thought about it, he knew that his times with Carole were great. But what did she mean when she said she thanked him for everything. And when he questioned her, she answered with a smile.

She never thanked him for sex. Then what? Does she think that he had something to do with the death of her husband? And now she has the business all to herself?

Chapter Sixteen
Mrs. Benson Interview

A follow-up meeting was scheduled with Carole Benson at the offices of Premier Equipment. After O'Brien and Harrington were greeted at the door by the receptionist, Clara, they were led to the office previously occupied by Charles Benson.

Carole Benson was sitting behind the desk. As the detectives walked in, they were greeted by Mrs. Benson, "Hello again, please have a seat."

The detectives seated themselves in the two chairs across from the desk, "Good afternoon Mrs. Benson," opened O'Brien.

"Hello, Mrs. Benson," followed Harrington.

"Thank you for agreeing to see us again," continued O'Brien. "As you can understand, we're still working all aspects of the investigation."

"Yes, thank you," responded Carole.

"We did have a few more questions for you. I should mention that we met with David Wilson," O'Brien began.

A serious look came over the face of Carole that

could not be hidden from the detectives.

"Were you and David close?" inquired O'Brien.

"Well, we worked together on the same projects, if that's what you mean," Carole tried to clarify.

"We were aware of that, but I wanted to ask you," O'Brien hesitated."Well this is a bit awkward, but did you ever feel that Mr. Wilson was taking a liking to you?"

"As I look back, and give it some thought, he did tell me that he thought that I appeared capable of running the business by myself. He commented that Charles was frequently out of the office, either golfing or at some other function, and the workload fell on my shoulders," Carole explained. "You know when he would say those things to me, I felt that he was trying to flatter me. I don't know if he was attempting to make me feel good or what."

"Again, Mrs. Benson, there are guidelines and obligations that we must follow when we are involved in a serious investigation. And this is certainly a serious investigation," explained O'Brien.

"I understand," said Carole.

"Then let me ask you directly. Did your relationship with David Wilson go beyond business?"

When O'Brien stopped talking, Carole put her face in her hands and leaned forward on the desk and began to cry. "I feel terrible. Charles was a good man. He built this business. He provided me with everything I needed."

O'Brien and Harrington said nothing, but remained seated and listened to Carole.

"But there were problems. Maybe there are in any marriage. He was older and his needs and desires became different from mine," she explained. "Then David appeared on the scene. He was strong and vibrant. I suddenly felt different when he was around me. I felt that I had life. Something that was lacking in me for a long time."

After a moment of silence, O'Brien said, "We appreciate your honesty and openness."

"I don't know," Carole went on. "Maybe I should have used my head. Handled things differently. David did come on pretty strong. And I was feeling vulnerable."

Again, the detectives sat quietly listening.

"He told me that we work well as a team. He said he would always be there to help me, no matter what. You don't think...?"

We're just handling the investigation," Harrington interjected. "Just gathering facts."

"Thank you Mrs. Benson. We appreciate your candor in a sensitive situation," said O'Brien. "We have no further questions."

With that, the detectives left the office.

As they drove away from the offices of Premier Equipment, they summarized and discussed the conversation just concluded.

O'Brien opened the discussion, "I guess you were right. There was some humpty dumpty going on."

"You mean rumpy pumpy?" Harrington tried to clarify.

"Okay, that too," concurred O'Brien with a grin. "I think we need to reconnect with David Wilson."

Chapter Seventeen
David Wilson

A telephone call was made by Detective Patrick O'Brien to David Wilson and the parties agreed to set up another meeting. As before, the meeting was scheduled to be at the Law Office of Thomas Finley. A follow up meeting by the detectives concerned David. He decided to discuss the situation with his roommate, Thomas Finley.

David told Tom that he needed to discuss a legal matter with him. Of course, Tom was thinking that one of David's counseling clients needed legal services—possibly an incorporation or litigation on a tax matter.

As they sat at the kitchen table in their apartment, David said to Tom, "I think I might need the use of your legal services."

"Okay, what type of client?" Tom asked.

"No. Actually I'm asking for your legal representation of me as the client," David clarified.

"Oh, really? What's the situation," Tom inquired.

"I have a client called Premier Equipment," David

began. "They lease and rent all types of equipment, primarily to contractors."

"I think you may have mentioned it to me in a previous discussion," Tom said.

"Well, the company was owned by a man named Charles Benson. His wife Carole worked with him in the business. I came across them one day while doing my cold calling activities," David explained.

"Okay," said Tom, following along.

"I was able to amend their prior tax returns and generate some pretty sizable tax refunds for them. Following those successful results, I started to analyze their accounting operations," detailed David.

"Sounds like a good client," said Tom, continuing to follow along.

"It is," confirmed David. "In doing the analyzing of their accounting practices, I worked with the wife of the owner, Carole. I'll tell you, she is a real knockout."

"What do you mean?" inquired Tom.

"Real good looking, with a great figure. Hard to take your eyes off her. We spent a lot of time together. We started to really enjoy each other's company."

Tom looked back at David with a serious look on his face.

David went on, "Well one thing led to another

and we got involved. We started seeing each other outside of the office on a regular basis."

"Not a good situation, considering this being a good client," Tom advised.

"You're right," David agreed. "Then comes the worst part."

"Her husband found out?" interjected Tom.

"No. But someone murdered him."

"What! Are you serious?" asked a surprised Tom.

"Yes. It happened about three weeks ago," said David.

"The police are doing an investigation. Two detectives came to the office to see me. Since he was my client, they were asking me questions about him, you know, what I knew about him and his activities, just a lot of general questions," David tried to explain.

"And," Tom asked. "Where do I come into this situation?"

"Now they called to set up a follow up meeting with me to ask me some additional questions," David explained.

"I agree that it would be best if you had legal representation in this matter, especially based on the situation that you just informed me about," explained Tom.

"I don't know what they want to ask me, you know, beyond what I already told them," David said.

"I'm not sure," answered Tom, "but you're going to have to be honest with them. If asked, you're going to have to be open with them about your relationship with the owner's wife."

"I guess so," agreed David.

"Of course. No doubt about it. If not, and they find that you're not being honest with them, then they will try to open other doors. They'll convince themselves that you're hiding something else."

At the scheduled time, Detectives O'Brien and Harrington arrived at the Office of Thomas Finley. They were led by the receptionist into the conference room where David and Tom were waiting. The detectives were surprised to see Tom there. He introduced himself as the attorney representing David.

"Mr. Wilson, thank you for agreeing to see us again," O'Brien opened. "We're continuing with our investigation into the death of Charles Benson. We recently met with Mrs. Benson at the office of Premier Equipment. Have you spoken to Mrs. Benson recently?"

"No I haven't," responded David.

"Well, Mrs. Benson was very open and forthright with us. She informed us that, outside of your business counseling services to Premier Equipment, the two of you have had a continuing relationship."

"That's true," answered David.

"You failed to mention that before when we met with you," O'Brien said.

"No," answered David. "You were previously asking me about Charles Benson and his clients."

O'Brien and Harrington looked at each other and then back at David. Then O'Brien stated, "She indicated that you were very aggressive and that she felt vulnerable."

"That's not quite true," answered David.

O'Brien continued, "She also stated that you told her that she could run the business herself without Mr. Benson. She further said that you told her that the two of you made a good team."

"That's just not accurate," defended David. "I have a hard time believing she said all that."

"What are you trying to imply?" Tom interjected.

"Nothing. We're just pursuing all aspects of our investigation," set forth O'Brien. "I think that will be all for now. Thank you for your time, gentlemen."

The two detectives got up from their seats, left the conference room, and then left the building.

After they left, David and Tom looked at each other for a moment. Then David spoke up, "I didn't say any of those things. They're trying to set me up for something I did not do."

"Well, they are looking at all aspects as they pursue their investigation," responded Tom.

"What happens now?" asked David.

"I don't know. But there's nothing that we need to do at this time. If you are contacted again, let me know immediately. Don't talk to them on your own, whether in person or on the phone," advised Tom.

"I can't believe Carole said any of those things," said an incredulous David. "I felt that we really cared about each other. I know that it's crazy to say this, but I felt that we were falling in love. We had deep feelings toward each other."

"You may not want to hear this, but what you are experiencing and expressing to me may not be a case of falling in love, but more likely you were falling in lust," cautioned Tom. "As your attorney, and looking out for your best interest, I'm advising you not to see Carole at this time. Not in person, not on the phone, not by email or text, No communication, whatsoever. Again it's in your best interest."

David said nothing further.

Chapter Eighteen
David's Investigation

David understood Tom's advice. He was speaking as an attorney—as David's attorney. But David felt that Tom did not see the situation in the same way that David was viewing it. Tom's advice to avoid and stay clear of Carole was logically correct from a legal standpoint. An attorney does not want his client to be in harm's way.

But Tom was not experiencing the emotions that David was feeling. David needed to sort out everything in his own mind. He didn't really know what Carole meant when she thanked him for everything. Did she really think that David had something to do with the death of Charlie?

David cared very much for her. In his mind, she felt that way about him. But there was no way that he wanted her to go on thinking that he could have committed a murder. If they had a future together, he couldn't have her thinking that way. There could be no future between them without her knowing the truth.

What continued to surface in David's mind was that Tom's legal advice to him was correct. He was directing David to follow his advice to protect his client and his friend. That was completely understood. However, in his mind, David could not stand by and wait for something to happen or something not to happen. He had to engage himself in an effort to find out the truth. He decided to see Carole.

David placed a call to Premier Equipment. As the call went through, he heard, "Premier Equipment, may I help you?"

"Hello Clara, this is David Wilson."

"Oh hello David, how are you?"

"Good. Is Carole in?"

"Yes, let me ring her."

"Hi David, how are you?

"Fine. I'd like to stop by to see you," he said.

"Should we meet for coffee?" she asked.

"No. I would like to meet you at Premier. I think it's best if we don't change any patterns relating to my services to Premier," he explained

"You think that's a good idea under the circumstances?" she inquired.

"Yes, absolutely. For anybody observing me or you, whether it be Clara or the police, I think it makes more sense to continue to show a professional relationship, rather than having it stopped abruptly," David continued, detailing his explanation.

"Okay, how about this afternoon, about one thirty?" she asked.

"Good, I'll see you there," David confirmed.

David arrived at their scheduled time and he and Carole met in her office with the door opened. He engaged in a business discussion in regular conversational tones. During their discussion, he suggested that he review the depreciation schedules for Premier Equipment, in which he commented that they were quite extensive and should be verified.

She agreed to get out the schedules for his review and have him set up in the conference room. She then informed him that she had an appointment at the spa later that afternoon. David was to look over the depreciation schedules while she was gone. He would then leave Premier, telling Clara that he would leave all the documents in the conference room.

Carole would not return to Premier that afternoon, as had been planned by the two of them. By arrangement, they were to meet at the coffee shop after the regular working hours.

The two met at the coffee shop as had been planned. David was sitting at a table in the back of the shop with two cups of coffee. Carole walked back and sat at the table with David.

"Should we move to a more private setting?" David asked.

"No, I don't think that would be a good idea at this time," Carole responded to the usual offer.

David, appearing somewhat surprised for a moment, then responded, "You're right. Maybe that would be best for now."

After engaging in some small talk, David got serious, "I'm really concerned about the detectives."

"I am too," responded Carole. "They are going to make every effort to solve it."

"I know, but I was very uncomfortable with the questions they were asking me. They didn't come out and say anything, but I felt they were almost implicating me because of the relationship that I have with you," David tried to explain.

Carole said nothing, but just looked at David and listened to him.

"Was Charlie having problems with anyone? Could there have been gambling debts or something that could have triggered some type of problems for Charlie?" David inquired.

"I'm not aware of anything like that, but in a way, Charlie was a very private person. He spent a lot of time out of the office, and a lot of time away from me," she tried to explain.

After some further inquiries regarding Charlie,

David and Carole ended their discussion and left. In parting, Carole said they would be in touch with each other. David could not help but feel that Carole appeared a little distant from him.

David did call Carole a week later. He said that he needed to see her. They arranged to meet in a shopping center parking lot. Carole then got into the car with David and he drove to the motel where they had met before.

When they went into the room, David asked Carole if she had heard anything regarding the investigation. Carole said she hadn't. Changing the subject, David told Carole that he missed seeing her and didn't want anything to change between them. As she started to undress, she then said that she appreciated everything that he was doing and everything he had done for her in the past.

Without any further discussion the two of them embraced and engaged in sex. However, to David, it seemed uncomfortable. He was feeling that Carole seemed to be going through the motions.

It was different. Shortly thereafter, they left the motel and David drove Carole back to her car.

As he drove away, his head became filled with many thoughts. Did Carole really suspect him of having something to do with the death of Charlie? Of course, she did meet with the detectives previously. Could she be working with them? Did the police suspect that David had something to do with the crime?

David started to play out the scenario in his mind. Here he was having sexual relations with the wife of a client. Subsequently, the husband is murdered.

He thought about any conversations he had with Carole, both now and before. His dancing thoughts centered on police stories that he had seen in movies. Could she have been wearing a wire or other listening or recording device? Realistically, no. If she had, it would have been the only thing she had on in the motel. She wore nothing else.

Moving to a position of more logic than emotion, David decided to follow Tom's legal advice. He should avoid having contacts with Carole—at least for now.

Chapter Nineteen
David's Dilemma

David was dealing with an assortment of emotions. He had feelings for Carole that he felt he couldn't just get over. At the same time he was feeling confused. What was her motivation? In his mind he kept thinking of what he could or would say to her. However, he needed to follow the advice of his attorney.

Tom was not only his attorney, but was also a friend. When he took a moment to think about the situation, he understood that Tom was looking at the situation logically. But David knew that he was thinking about the situation emotionally.

One day David decided to see if Carole was at the offices of Premier Equipment. But how could he do that. If he drove to the area, his car would be recognized, having been there so many times. Even Clara would notice the car. So, he decided to rent a car for a few days. He could then drive by the area, wearing some type of cap, and not be recognized.

The location of the rental car office was a few blocks from his apartment. He walked to that location. He rented a car and drove to his destination—Premier Equipment. As planned, he wore an old baseball cap that he had received at a promotion a few years earlier.

As he drove past the Premier Equipment office, he could see Carole's car parked behind the building. He waited for a while and eventually left. He killed some time running some errands—post office, bank and an office supply store. Then he decided to drive back to Premier Equipment.

Again he waited in his rental car. He looked through his material that he had just purchased at the office supply store, and then thumbed through a book that he had in the car. Not deeply engrossed in anything, he kept looking up at the office building. All at once he saw Carole emerge from the office and get into her car. He made every effort to hide his face with his hand and pulled down the cap over his face.

After he heard Carole's car drive by, he started the rental car and proceeded to follow her. Not surprisingly, she drove to the gym where she had gone frequently for her exercise routine. Although she was usually there for an hour or an hour and a half, David decided to just sit in his car.

Surprisingly, within ten minutes, Carole walked out of the facility. With her was the trainer that she had been seen with before. They walked over and got into what must have been his car.

Again, David was careful not to be seen. He watched as the car drove off. He couldn't help himself. He had to follow them. This went on for a couple of miles. Then, unbelievably, the car entered the familiar motel parking lot. David stopped his car on the street. The trainer emerged from the car and went into the motel office.

After a few minutes, the trainer came out of the office. He then drove the car to the end of the aisle and parked it at one of the designated spaces. The two of them, Carole and the trainer, got out of the car and went into the motel unit. David felt that his head was throbbing and his blood boiling. He was having a difficult time processing what he was seeing.

David started the car and drove away. He needed to drive away and attempt to clear his head. As he drove away, he felt that he needed to know who this guy was. He drove to the gym, parked the car and went into the gym. He was greeted at the counter by one of the attendants. "Can I help you," she asked.

"Yes, I was referred to your gym, and specifically to one of the trainers, but I don't know his name," he answered.

"Well we have several trainers at the spa. All of them are excellent physical trainers."

"I was told that he was about six foot two and probably weighed about two hundred pounds. They said he was good looking and had dark hair," described David.

"Oh, you mean Matt Simmons," she responded

"Okay. Is he here?" David inquired.

"No, but he should be back in about an hour."

"Alright, I'll be back later," David said and turned away immediately before the attendant could ask him anything further.

David got into his car and drove away. As he drove away, he decided to drive back to the motel. As he arrived at the motel entrance, he could see the trainer's car still parked in the same space as before. Then he decided to position his car where he could see when someone would emerge from the motel unit.

As he waited, he took out his cell phone and started to position it to where he could record someone coming out. He waited a while. Then, he saw the door open. He got his cell phone positioned. Then as he saw the trainer, Matt Simmons, and Carole walk out of the motel unit, he recorded it. At that moment, he didn't think about what he was going to do next, but somehow he needed to have that scene recorded. Maybe, if he thought he awoke from this terrible dream, he would need this to bring him back to reality.

After Carole and Matt Simmons drove away, David started his car and left the area. He was heading back home. In his mind, David determined that his escapade of his investigation showed results—not what he wanted to see, but results nevertheless.

It was early in the afternoon. David returned the rental car and went back to his apartment. He needed to be alone.

As he had planned, David spent the rest of the afternoon at his apartment. Much time was spent staring at the ceiling. He eventually dozed off. He was awakened when Tom arrived home.

"You're here early," Tom greeted him.

"Yeah, I didn't have a lot of places to go today," answered David.

After Tom sat down in the living room to look at the newspaper, David sat in another chair across from Tom. "When you have a minute, I need to talk to you," he opened.

"Okay. What's going on?" Tom inquired.

David then leaned forward, ready to tell his detailed story. "I need to say some things and I need you to hear it all."

With that, Tom put down the newspaper. David now had his complete attention. David then laid out in detail the events of the day, including the information he obtained about Matt Simmons'

115

name and the recorded evidence showing the motel departure by Carole and Simmons.

Tom looked at him and said, "When I wanted you to stay away from Carole, it was in your own best interest. I know this has been difficult for you. At the same time I can only imagine what you're going through."

"Thank you," responded David.

"What Now?" asked Tom.

"The police are looking at me for something I didn't do. It might be objectively easy for someone to sit idly by and say that they have nothing to tie me to any crime. Nothing to worry about," David explained.

"I hear what you're saying," said Tom, following along.

"But it's not my nature to sit by and wait for something to happen, or something not to happen," David went on. "I want to go to the police and show them what I have."

"I follow you," said Tom.

"And I'd like you to go with me, as my attorney," David reasoned. "I would feel much better under those circumstances."

"Except, I think it's best if I go myself and present the evidence you've obtained. I don't want them asking you any more questions at this time," Tom explained. "I'll contact them and set up a meeting."

Tom called Detective O'Brien, reminding him that he was the attorney for David Wilson. He told O'Brien that he would like to meet with them regarding the investigation of the murder of Charles Benson.

Detective Patrick O'Brien made arrangements for himself and Detective Steve Harrington to meet with Thomas Finley. Even though the subject matter had not been stated, both O'Brien and Harrington anticipated that Finley might be coming to meet with them to discuss David Wilson's involvement in the crime.

As the three individuals sat down in a conference room at the police station, O'Brien opened the discussion, looking at Attorney Thomas Finley and said, "Mr. Finley, you called for this meeting, what did you want to discuss?"

"My client was very upset in our last meeting with the characterization of his relationship with Mrs. Benson," Tom opened. "He was up front with the investigation in admitting to a relationship with Mrs. Benson. However, he was presented with a situation in which he was shown to be very aggressive and his ultimate ambition was to end up with Mrs. Benson, with Mr. Benson not being in the picture.

"We didn't say that," responded O'Brien.

"No, but putting the pieces all together, Mr.

Wilson certainly felt like he was a person of interest by the police in the investigation of the death of Charles Benson."

O'Brien and Harrington sat there and did not add anything further to the discussion.

"Being very uncomfortable with the situation, Mr. Wilson, without any advice from me, decided to do some investigating on his own," Tom went on, laying out his story.

Again, O'Brien and Harrington, still saying nothing, appeared to lean forward, waiting for a story to unfold.

"Mr. Wilson has a video from his cell phone that reveals some information that you might find interesting," Tom continued. He then opened his briefcase and produced David's cell phone.

With that introduction, Tom showed the cell phone images to the two detectives. They viewed what was shown, but said nothing.

"As you can see," Finley said, "Mrs. Benson is clearly seen entering the motel on the date indicated. The other individual is Matt Simmons. He is a trainer at the local spa where Mrs. Benson goes for her physical workouts."

"This is obviously an arranged meeting to conduct a physical workout at an offsite location," commented Tom with a sly grin. "You may consider expanding your investigation, detectives. My client,

David Wilson, just does not appreciate being a target or a person of interest. He had nothing to do with the death of Charles Benson. In spite of my advice to him, he refused to sit by in an idle manner. Even though he and Mrs. Benson were having a relationship, he had no involvement in the crime."

"Anything else, Mr. Finley?" O'Brien asked.

"Nothing further," responded Tom.

"Then we'll conclude this meeting," said O'Brien.

After Tom left, Detectives O'Brien and Harrington sat down to discuss the recent events.

"That was eye opening and very revealing," Harrington opened.

"Yes," responded O'Brien. "I can't help thinking how Mrs. Benson reacted when we confronted her about a relationship with David Wilson. Remember how she cried, saying how vulnerable she was, and how aggressive Wilson was with her?"

"What do you think?' asked Harrington. "Could it be that she happened to bump into another very aggressive dude two weeks after her husband was murdered?" he asked, revealing a sly grin.

"I think we need to have a chat with this trainer. What did he say his name was," asked O'Brien.

"Simmons, Matt Simmons," answered Harrington.

"Yes, I agree. We should talk to him. Let's have a go at it."

Chapter Twenty
Matt Simmons

Detectives O'Brien and Harrington drove to the location of the spa where Matt Simmons worked as a trainer. They walked in and were greeted by the receptionist. They asked to see Matt Simmons. When asked, they told her it was a private matter. She then called for the trainer.

When Matt Simmons walked up to the front, they asked if there was a place that they could speak privately. He said that outside the spa was best. After they walked out, the detectives told him that they had some questions to ask him about the death of Charles Benson, who was the husband of one of his clients, Carole Benson.

They offered to speak with him inside, or it might be better for him if they met at the police station. It would draw less attention there. They told him that a discussion at the spa may generate questions from others that may be uncomfortable to him. He agreed and they set up a meeting at the police station that afternoon.

Matt Simmons arrived at the police station for his scheduled meeting with the police detectives. Detective O'Brien met him in the lobby and led him to a conference room where they were joined by Detective Harrington. O'Brien opened the interview with, "Did you know the deceased, Charles Benson?'

"No, not really," Simmons answered.

"When you say 'no, not really,' what do you mean?" asked O'Brien.

"Well, we never met. But Carole, his wife, is one of my trainees at the spa," Simmons responded. "She used to talk to me about her husband. In that way I kind of knew the kind of person that he was."

Harrington looked up after that response and asked, "Really, and what kind of a person was he?"

"Not very good. I would have to say he was abusive to Carole."

"How do you know that?" asked O'Brien.

"She worked out at the spa with me. We talked. She told me that it was a relief to be at the spa with someone who was not abusive to her," Simmons went on.

"You were at the spa with her on a regular basis. Did you see any bruises on her?" asked O'Brien.

"No, but abuse doesn't necessarily have to be physical. He just wasn't good for her," Simmons answered

"And did you feel that you were the right man for her?" inquired O'Brien.

"That's really none of your business."

"Oh, but I think it might be," responded O'Brien.

"Is this where I'm supposed to say I want a lawyer?" Simmons asked.

"Do you feel you want an attorney?" inquired O'Brien.

"I don't need no fuckin' lawyer. I can handle this myself," responded Simmons.

"Okay, then. We have no further questions. Thank you for your time. That's all for now," said O'Brien."

Simmons got up off his chair, said nothing, and left the conference room and police station, never looking again at the detectives.

"I'm just playing this out in my mind," said O'Brien. "After seeing the recent visuals we saw, I'm seeing Mrs. Benson in a different light. What if Mrs. Benson's motivation was to take over the business by herself. She couldn't do it with a divorce. Her husband started the business and built it to where it is today. In a divorce, he would retain the business. A divorce just wouldn't work for her."

"That's true," agreed Harrington.

"And Wilson was the object in her first approach. They hooked up together, but she realized that he would not be the one to eliminate her husband,"

O'Brien continued to reason

"And then Simmons became the perfect object of her desired results," Harrington responded in concurrence with the theory.

"This lady has the looks, the figure. Realistically, all the tools to persuade someone like Simmons," concluded O'Brien.

"Yes, she does have all the tools, and most clearly, she knows how to use them. There is one thing that struck me right from the start of this investigation," said Harrington.

"What's that?" inquired O'Brien.

"I listened to the tape of the telephone call from Mrs. Benson on the night of the murder. She was saying that she had tried to reach her husband at home and at the office. She said she was afraid that he might have fallen or had a medical problem. You know, these things could have happened at home or at the office," explained Harrington.

"What struck you as unusual?" O'Brien inquired.

In response, Harrington noted that, "She seemed to be directing the police to check the office instead of the home. Almost like she knew where the police could find her husband."

"And the call came in at what time?" asked O'Brien.

"It was ten thirty from Scottsdale, Arizona. By the way, where in Arizona is Scottsdale? Harrington inquired.

"It's in the Phoenix area. That place drives me crazy," said O'Brien. "How so?" asked Harrington.

"I went on a mini vacation to Phoenix a few years ago, around Thanksgiving," O'Brien started to explain. "I called to make a reservation at a hotel in October. Before I got off the phone with the hotel reservations, I asked them what time it was there in Phoenix. They told me that it was the same time as California. She gave me their time and I verified it, looking at my watch. It was the same as our time in California. I thought great. I won't have to change the time on my watch when I go there."

"And?" said Harrington, patiently listening to O'Brien's long winded and unexciting tale

"Then, when I went to Phoenix around Thanksgiving, I had dinner one night and then decided to go back to the hotel room to watch one of the new police programs, *Major Crimes*. It came on at ten o'clock."

"And, then?" said Harrington, continuing to listen, being politely patient.

"Well, I turned on the television in the hotel room and some newscaster thanked the viewers for watching the evening news. What? How can that be? It was only nine thirty. I discovered later that when I made the reservations in October, California was on daylight savings time. Later California went back to standard time. Arizona never changes. They stay on Mountain Time year round. Not only that, but prime time in Arizona is seven to ten while California is eight to eleven. Bottom line? According to my watch, which was on California time, *Major Crimes* came on at eight o'clock, and the late news was on from nine to nine thirty."

"I'll be sure to keep that in mind, but that should be a lesson to you," said Harrington. "When you go on holiday, treat it as a holiday. Don't do the routine things you would do at the end of a work day"

"How did I get started on this anyway?" asked O'Brien.

"We were talking about the time Mrs. Benson's call came to the police station," responded Harrington.

"Oh, that's right," said O'Brien. "I guess I got a little off track."

Harrington said nothing, but just smiled back at O'Brien.

Detective Steve Harrington arrived earlier than normal at the police station the next morning. To his surprise, Detective Patrick O'Brien was on his second cup of coffee, poring over some notes in his folder.

"You're here early," said Harrington.

"Yes. I've been thinking over our discussion about this Benson murder," said O'Brien. "I've been reviewing my notes and going over the scenario of events. Like I said yesterday, I'm looking at Mrs. Benson a little differently now."

"Yes," concurred Harrington.

"She's married to this older dude. Life is getting a little stale. Maybe boring in her mind. She's got a lot going for her, you know, with her looks and appearance. And there's this very successful business at hand," O'Brien summarized.

"And this old man of a husband is standing in the way of her desires," Harrington added.

"Yeah. She may have been thinking about this for a while," O'Brien continued. "First this Wilson guy arrives on the scene. Feelers were sent out by her to Wilson, but that wasn't going to stick. She realized that he was not the answer."

"Then she hooks up with this bruiser Simmons. He has the brawn, but lacks the brains," Harrington filled in. "An easy mark for her. Very easily persuaded. He was needed for a purpose, and then poof, he's out of the picture. There's nothing I could see long term for those two. I wonder if he has a record?"

"No, he's clean. I checked that when I came in this morning," concluded O'Brien. "But I've got an idea. Let's get another cup of coffee."

"My first, but I'm up to it," responded Harrington.

O'Brien and Harrington sat down with their coffees and O'Brien laid out his plan. Since O'Brien was moving toward his retirement, a uniformed officer on the staff at Baytown Beach had been working part time with him. He was being groomed to replace O'Brien after his retirement.

O'Brien's plan was to have this newbie go through the motions and go to the spa where Matt Simmons worked. Whether it was under the guise of a future membership or if he actually had to join didn't matter. His assignment was to get some article used by Simmons to gather the necessary DNA. It could be a towel or rag, or whatever would do the trick.

The plan was executed. The newbie was anxious to cooperate with the undercover investigation. O'Brien didn't know whether the newbie joined the spa or not. It didn't matter to him. In a short time, a towel used by Simmons, was produced. Mission accomplished. The item was immediately sent to the lab.

It had not been previously disclosed outside of the inner circle of the police, but the coroner was able to find some skin samples under the finger nails of Charles Benson during the autopsy. About three weeks after the towel of Simmons was taken, the results were received from the lab. It was a match to Matt Simmons.

127

After Detectives O'Brien and Harrington received the results from the coroner, they were convinced they had the person that murdered Charles Benson. But the two of them felt troubled.

"Could it be that Simmons was so upset that his married girlfriend was an abused woman?" O'Brien asked. "I think I could almost answer that question myself. Not really."

"As we could see, Simmons is a perfect physical specimen," described Harrington. "He's good looking, big, brawny, muscular, and he knows it. Did I miss something in that description?"

"That's his physical appearance. It's great, but he's a little lacking in his smarts," responded O'Brien. "He's one of those guys who's led around by his dick. The bulk of his brains is in his penis."

"That would be a perfect target for someone like Mrs. Benson," added Harrington.

"We need to make an arrest of Matt Simmons," said O'Brien. "But we need to do this the right way. We can't let somebody get away with murder when we're convinced otherwise."

"I'm on the exact same page with you on this, governor," responded Harrington.

Detectives O'Brien and Harrington proceeded to make an arrest of Matt Simmons. However, this time Simmons retained the services of an attorney. He and his attorney were present when they went into the interrogation room at the police station.

Before entering the interrogation room, O'Brien commented to Harrington, "In spite of what he said in our last visit, I guess Simmons found a fuckin' lawyer that he didn't need before."

"Yes, but judging from his level of brilliance, this may be a benefit to us," responded Harrington.

O'Brien and Harrington entered the room and introductions proceeded among the parties.

"Mr. Simmons, we know you had an encounter with the deceased, Charles Benson, you know, the husband of your girlfriend," O'Brien said, opening the interrogation. "We have evidence of a struggle. We don't have to waste a lot of time here. Do you have a statement for us?"

Simmons looked at his attorney. Following a nod by his attorney, Simmons opened with, "I didn't know Benson, but I went to see him to talk to him about his abuse of Carole."

'So what happened?" asked O'Brien.

"We got into a discussion. It became heated and he tried to force me out of his office. There was a struggle and in self defense, I defended myself," answered Simmons.

"That will never fly with a jury," said O'Brien. He was grabbed from the back. According to the coroner, brute force was applied and his neck was broken."

"I'm going to level with you. Records show that Mrs. Benson called you twice that afternoon from Scottsdale, Arizona, O'Brien explained. "And after you made a telephone call to her hotel, she made another call back to you."

"We spoke about another appointment when she arrived back in California," Simmons answered.

"Come on, Mr. Simmons, you're being duped by your girlfriend," interjected Harrington. "She was not an abused woman. She was using you as her tool. As an instrument to get rid of her husband. It worked. She now has the business all to herself now that you took care of her husband for her."

Simmons said nothing, but only stared back at Harrington.

"We're going to let you in on a secret. Your girlfriend was entertaining another bloke before you arrived on the scene. They were carrying on at your same motel on a regular basis—maybe even your same room. He didn't take the bait to eliminate her husband and let her have the business."

Simmons continued to stare, but said nothing.

Harrington went on, "Now you're going to go to prison to think about everything for a long time. And you know what? Your girlfriend is no doubt trolling around for your replacement. It wouldn't take much. With her looks and that figure, it won't be long before she spreads her legs and is ready for the next dude."

Simmons said nothing, but was becoming extremely agitated.

His attorney stepped in and said, "Could you give me a minute with my client?"

"Yes," answered Harrington, as he and O'Brien got up and left the room.

A short time later, the detectives were called back into the interrogation room. The attorney asked if they could discuss some accommodation for his client if he cooperated with them. They said they would do what was in their power.

Subsequently, Simmons confessed to the murder of Charles Benson. He explained how Carole had worked out the details. He admitted that he was confused as to when and where he would confront Charles Benson. He tried to get the home address, but Carole angrily said to confront him at the office when the receptionist was not there. Hence that explained the telephone calls between Simmons and Arizona. A confession with all the details was produced.

After the interrogation was over, O'Brien told Harrington, "You really got to him, didn't you?"

'Yes, he's not the smartest guy around, but he was smart enough to know when he was getting screwed," answered Harrington. "Both literally and figuratively."

Chapter Twenty-One
Prosecution

Following the confinement of Matt Simmons, Detectives O'Brien and Harrington were ready to proceed with the next phase of the murder investigation. They would meet with, and present, the case to the prosecutor at the district attorney's office. This was a routine procedure. However, in many cases, the procedure did not seem routine.

They had a confession from Matt Simmons. However, they needed to convince the prosecutor that the criminal activity included the role played by Carole Benson. Homicide detectives know that enough evidence has to be presented for the prosecutor to pursue a case. Not just pursue a case, but to win a case.

A prosecutor has a duty and an obligation to evaluate the circumstances to determine whether or not a crime has been committed. Their role is not just one to arbitrarily present a case and see if a judge or jury finds the individual guilty or not guilty.

Generally, a prosecutor will not pursue a case unless he or she is confident that they can obtain a guilty verdict as a result of their efforts. Resumes of prosecutors will include the convictions achieved. And veteran prosecutors will always present the number of cases where the death penalty has been achieved. At the same time criminal defense attorneys will display their success in acquittals, and with the number of cases where their client avoided the death penalty. Scorecards are kept.

Detectives O'Brien and Harrington were quite aware of the challenge that was lying ahead of them in pursuing the prosecution of Carole Benson. Their story had to be compelling for the prosecutor.

They had the anticipated testimonial evidence of the relationship and the discussions that Mrs. Benson had with David Wilson. They did have the prosecution witness, Matt Simmons. He was their key witness, or as the detectives said, their ace in the case. However, the two detectives were experienced enough to realize that Simmons, using the card game vernacular, may not be an ace, but instead might be a card of a much lower value. The prosecution team needed to play their cards effectively.

Either way, O'Brien and Harrington were each convinced that Carole Benson was ultimately responsible for the death of her husband, Charles

Benson. Their job was to convince the prosecutor of the same.

Detectives O'Brien and Harrington met with the prosecutor, Lester Carpenter, to present their case. Following their initial meeting, the supervising prosecutor was brought in. Eventually, the discussions included the district attorney. This was no ordinary homicide case.

Many meetings and discussions ensued, including the participation of the attorney for Matt Simmons, regarding the sought after concessions for his client, Matt Simmons. His attorney was pursuing a plea of manslaughter. The prosecution was pushing for a plea of second degree. Simmons' attorney presented the argument that Simmons was stepping in on behalf of a battered spouse—not necessarily that she was one, but that was his belief.

He further tried to persuade them that Simmons went to see Charles Benson and confront him with the abuse of the woman that he loved. The situation got out of hand. A struggle ensued between Benson and Simmons which resulted in the death of Benson.

Considering the totality of the situation and weighing the presentation of O'Brien and Harrington and the persuasive argument of Simmons' attorney, the prosecution team became convinced that Carole Benson was responsible for the death of her husband, Charles Benson. They decided to accept a plea of manslaughter from Matt Simmons. Their complete focus evolved into the pursuit of the conviction of Carole Benson.

Detectives O'Brien and Harrington had their marching orders. Following the finalization of the prosecutors' plans to pursue the conviction of Carole Benson, they drove to the offices of Premier Equipment. As they entered the office, they could see that there was no receptionist to greet them.

From her office, Carole Benson emerged, appearing to be surprised at the visit of the two detectives.

"Good afternoon gentlemen. What can I do for you?"

"Good afternoon, Mrs. Benson. You're under arrest for the murder of Charles Benson."

Chapter Twenty-Two
Legal Proceedings

If not shocking, Carole Benson's arrest had to be completely surprising. After she was taken into custody, not unexpectedly, she was able to retain the services of one of the leading criminal defense attorneys in the county. With her financial holdings and business interests, she was able to make bail. She was not considered a flight risk.

Her attorney made efforts to move matters along at a brisk pace. During a preliminary hearing, the prosecution presented Detective O'Brien and Detective Harrington as witnesses. However, little was presented by her attorney. As a result, the matter was set for trial in a relatively short period of time.

During an evidentiary hearing, the prosecutors were stymied in their efforts to present David Wilson as a prosecution witness. They were trying to show a pattern used by Carole Benson to persuade someone to carry out her plan for the demise of her husband.

However, Carole Benson's skillful attorney

argued effectively that, if presented in court, there was the danger of convicting a person of murder on the basis of her extramarital activities. The judge agreed. David Wilson's testimony was not allowed.

Eventually, the date for the trial had arrived. The impaneled jury consisted of seven men and five women. Prosecution witnesses Detectives O'Brien and Harrington testified about the results of their investigative work. They explained how their testimonies led to the arrest and subsequent confession of Matt Simmons.

The prosecutions' key witness, Matt Simmons, was called to the stand. Following the preliminary and routine questions, the prosecuting attorney, Les Carpenter, began to zero in on the key components in the case against Carole Benson.

After the confession was marked for evidence, the prosecutor, Les Carpenter, presented it to Simmons.

"Do you recognize this document?" Carpenter asked.

"Yes"

"Tell the jury what it is," pursued Carpenter

"It's my confession."

"To what," pressed Carpenter.

"To killing Charles Benson."

"Were you truthful when you wrote that confession?" asked Carpenter.

"Yes I was."

"Do you confirm that you committed the murder of Charles Benson?" asked Carpenter.

"What do you mean, confirm?" Simmons questioned as his eyebrows were furrowed.

"Did you in fact kill Charles Benson?" Carpenter tried to clarify.

"Yes, I did."

"Did you know Charles Benson?" Carpenter continued.

"No."

"Then why did you kill him?" asked Carpenter.

"I was in love with his wife. We loved each other. We planned it together. We had to. She was suffering from an abusive husband," Simmons tried to explain.

"Are you saying that his wife, the defendant, Carole Benson, planned the murder with you?" continued Carpenter.

"Yes. For us to be together, it was the only way. She said that if she asked for a divorce, he would kill her," Simmons went on.

"Was this a plan by Mrs. Benson for you to carry out while she was out of town?" asked Carpenter.

"Yes. I went to see Benson. I thought that maybe I could explain to him that Carole and I were in love and he might understand. Killing him might not have been necessary," Simmons explained.

"Then what happened?" questioned Carpenter.

"He became irate. He told me to get out of his office. Things got out of hand and we struggled. In the struggle, he was stronger than I thought. I think I was trying to defend myself when I actually broke his neck. He wasn't moving. I left the office after that."

"And then what did you do?" asked Carpenter.

"I called Carole in Arizona. That's where she was staying that night,"

"Did you tell her what happened?" questioned Carpenter.

"I just said it was done."

"And what did she say?" asked Carpenter.

"She told me to stay at home. She would call me when she got back from Arizona."

"Did Carole Benson call you later?" asked Carpenter.

"No. I never heard from her again, or saw her again. Until today. I felt betrayed."

"No further questions," Carpenter said, addressing the court.

The judge then looked to the attorney at the defense side, "Counselor, cross examination?"

"Yes your honor," responded Mark Edwards, the defense attorney for Carole Benson.

"Mr. Simmons, where did you meet the defendant, Carole Benson?" he asked the witness.

"She was a client at the spa where I am employed as a trainer," responded Simmons.

"Did you find her to be an attractive woman?"

"Yes I did."

"And did you pursue a relationship with Mrs. Benson, even though she was a student of yours," questioned Mark Edwards.

"Objection," snapped Les Carpenter, "she was not a student of Simmons or the spa."

"I'll allow the question," responded the judge. "Objection overruled. Please answer the question, Mr. Simmons.

"Well, we kind of hit it off."

"Hit it off? Didn't you in fact pursue a relationship with Mrs. Benson?"

"No, it wasn't like that. We took a liking to each other. It eventually became serious," explained Simmons.

"Isn't it true that you found yourself obsessed with Mrs. Benson and you were troubled that her husband was standing in the way of your relationship with Mrs. Benson?"

"No, we just enjoyed each other's company. I looked forward to her coming to the spa and having the opportunity to be with her," explained an irritated Simmons.

""And you felt that you, on your own, had to take Mr. Benson out of the picture to enable you to have

140

Mrs. Benson all to yourself?" As Mark Edwards pursued his cross examination of Simmons.

"No. Carole told me that she had been an abused woman. She feared her husband. She told me that if I didn't take care of things, then she would be a dead woman." Simmons answered.

"Mr. Simmons, let's end this fantasy," said Edwards. "Wasn't this a creation in your own mind? Isn't it true that you were bound and determined to have Mrs. Benson for yourself and the only way that this could happen was for you to eliminate Mr. Benson?"

"No. She told me I had to kill her husband or I would never see her alive again," Simmons said.

"No further questions," Edwards expressed to the judge.

"Redirect Mr. Carpenter?' asked the judge.

"Yes, your honor," responded Carpenter.

"Mr. Simmons, you stated that you and Mrs. Benson were in love. Is that correct?" asked Carpenter.

"Yes."

"Did Carole Benson ask you to kill her husband?"

"Yes she did."

"No further questions," said Carpenter.

"It is almost noon," said the judge. "We'll reconvene after the lunch break at one thirty."

Carole Benson told her attorney, Mark Edwards,

that she needed to talk to him. The two of them went into one of the private rooms used at the courthouse for attorney client discussions.

"Yes, did you have a question?" Mark Edwards asked Carole.

"No, not a question. But I've decided that I want to testify on my own behalf," Carole told Edwards.

"I don't think that's a good idea," explained Edwards.

"I watched the jury as Matt was testifying. I think it is necessary. I need to do it," Carole emphasized.

"I can see that I'm not going to be able to talk you out of this. You realize that the prosecution will cross examine you," he explained.

"I realize that. I'll be ready."

As the court reconvened, defense attorney, Mark Edwards, asked the judge if the attorneys could approach the bench. He told the judge that his client, Carole Benson, would be called as a witness.

The judge asked the prosecuting attorney, Les Carpenter if a brief recess was needed before the witness was called to the stand. Carpenter said he did need that recess. A brief recess was called. The jury exited the courtroom for the duration of the recess.

O'Brien got word from the prosecutors that Carole Benson was going to testify on her own behalf. It was openly obvious to all that her testimony was against the advice of Mark Edwards. However, it was her case and that was her decision.

O'Brien and Harrington waited in the hallway of the courtroom during the recess. O'Brien told Harrington that Carole Benson was going to testify.

"Are you serious?" responded Harrington.

"Yes. That could be her kiss of death, so to speak," commented O'Brien.

"I recall a case in England that one of my colleagues was involved in," offered Harrington. "The bloke was a widower who was accused of murdering his mother in law. After her death he would be rewarded with an inheritance," he explained. "There was little evidence that he murdered her. But the prosecutor was goading him to confess to the crime. He obviously refused, of course. However, for some reason, he decided to be a witness in his own case. We believed that he wanted to show up the prosecutor. His barrister was beside himself. But as good as the barrister was, he could not convince the bloke not to testify. He told his barrister that, in effect, he wanted to tell the prosecutor to take his case and stick it up his jumper."

"His what?" asked O'Brien.

"Well, I think you get the drift," Harrington explained.

"How did it turn out," O'Brien asked.

"The bloke did testify. As I said, there was little evidence to convict him. But as he engaged in his banter with the prosecutor, it must have appeared to the jury, by his display of cleverness, that he likely did poison his mother in law."

"Wow. That's interesting. Well, we'll have to see what happens in this case," reasoned O'Brien.

"Yes. It'll be interesting," said Harrington

After the recess, the court reconvened and Carole Benson was called to the witness stand where she was sworn in. On direct examination, her defense attorney, Mark Edwards, asked several routine questions before getting into the significant parts of her testimony.

She spoke of her background as a young girl working her way through school while pursuing many part time jobs in the process. She met her husband while working for an office supply firm calling on businesses to sell products.

Charles Benson, twenty plus years her senior, had recently been divorced. He took a liking to Carole and admired her style in selling the products offered by her company. She was aggressive, but in an admirable way, he would later tell her.

Carole turned down Charles when he asked her to go out to dinner. She said she felt uncomfortable in what she perceived as a date with one of her customers. She knew that her company would frown upon such activity.

But Charles pursued. He convinced her that a lunch meeting would be completely appropriate. This would enable them to discuss his various business needs of the products in a comfortable format.

Eventually, they were seeing more of each other and a relationship was developing. Charles told her that he liked her style and her business acumen. Eventually, he offered her a position with his company with a lucrative starting salary. Seeing the opportunity to move ahead in the business world, Carole accepted the position.

After a year or so, Carole found herself falling in love with Charles. A few months later the two would marry. Carole enjoyed the business activities and the benefits of a successful business operation. However, after a few years, Carole found herself married to a man who started to consume alcohol and was out of the office on a regular basis. She was running the business and she found Charles to be critical of the way she was handling the business activities.

"When your marriage reached that situation, what did you do?" asked Mark Edwards in direct examination.

"I continued to work hard at the business. The

last thing that I wanted was a failed marriage," she answered.

"Did you think about a divorce or a separation?"

"No. I would not give up on something that I believed in. That's the way I felt about our marriage," explained Carole. "There was hope that things would work out. I was certainly going to do everything I could to make that happen."

"What do you feel kept you going with that belief?" Edwards continued.

"I would look for some relief from my stress," said Carole. "It was at that time that I joined the spa. The physical activities were a release from any stress that I was incurring. I was able to feel good about myself."

"Is that where you met Matt Simmons?" asked Edwards.

"Yes. He was one of their trainers that the spa had assigned to me. He would work with me on different techniques and activities that helped with my muscle tone. It also was a great stress reliever."

"Did you become close with Matt Simmons?"

"Yes. And maybe that was a mistake. But I blame myself for that," responded Carole.

"What do you mean by that?"

"What I mean is that the spa was a great escape for me. It relieved my stress and I was feeling good about myself, despite the problems I was having in my marriage," Carole explained.

"But you said that maybe that was a mistake," pursued Mark Edwards. "What did you mean by a mistake?"

"As I said, it was an escape for me," she continued to explain. "I found Matt to be an understanding person. I opened up to him regarding some of the marital problems and the fact that I was so comfortable being at the spa. He was good company. But maybe I was too open about my problems at home."

"How did you feel that opening up to him was the wrong thing to do?" pressed Mark Edwards.

"I was becoming very close to Matt. He was inside my head. I felt that he knew so much about me. With my marriage problems, I was feeling very vulnerable. Matt was there and I was feeling comfortable with him," she explained.

"Was a relationship developing between you and Matt Simmons?" asked Edwards.

"As much as I did not want that to happen, it did. Matt would tell me that I deserved better treatment and care because I was a good person. He said that he could make me feel good. Before I could get any control of my emotions, we became involved in a sexual relationship," Carole rationalized.

"Were you in love with Matt Simmons?" asked Edwards.

"No. I was vulnerable, and eventually in over my head emotionally, said Carole.

"Did you ask Matt to cause harm to your husband, Charles Benson?" Edwards asked directly.

"No. Of course not. I would never do that," Carole responded. "I worked hard to save my marriage," Carole responded. "After I found that Charles was murdered, I was feeling guilty."

"Why did you feel guilty?" asked Edwards

"Because Matt must have thought that our relationship was more than what it was. To this day, I have difficulty coming to grips with what he must have thought was between us."

"Is there anything else that you would like to tell us?" asked Edwards.

"I am just sorry that Matt had the thoughts that he did. It cost Charles his life."

"No further questions, your honor," said Edwards.

"Cross examination, Mr. Carpenter," asked the judge.

"Yes," responded Carpenter.

"As he got up from his chair, he looked at Carole Benson.

"Mrs. Benson, do you recall conversations with Matt Simmons regarding how your life would be different without your husband, Charles Benson?" asked Carpenter.

"As I said, it was a mistake to tell Matt about my personal life and how the spa visits relieved my stress. But I never discussed anything like you're trying to insinuate," she responded.

"No insinuation. I'm just asking about the plans you had with Matt Simmons," responded Carpenter.

"There were no plans," she responded briskly.

"Are you trying to tell us that Matt Simmons took it upon himself to bring about the death of your husband?" asked Carpenter.

"As I said, I was in an emotional situation. I'm not going to tell you that I had no control of my relationship with Matt Simmons. But, Mr. Carpenter, do you really think that I would involve myself with somebody like Matt Simmons to plan a scheme like you're suggesting?" she asked.

"No further questions, your honor," offered the prosecuting attorney, Les Carpenter.

Closing arguments were presented, which were followed by jury instructions from the judge. The jury was then ready for their deliberations.

There was the usual nervousness by all parties and their attorneys. Had Matt Simmons been that credible in his testimony? Or did he read the situation wrongly? Did he commit an act with a dual purpose—giving relief to a woman that he was in love with, and enabling him to get his desired woman?

Was Carole convincing in her testimony, despite being advised against doing so by her attorney? Was there a reasonable doubt created in the minds of the jury in the case against Carole Benson?

The attorneys were engaged in second guessing themselves regarding the approach and handling of the case. Should things have been done differently?

Deliberations by the jury seemed to be taking a long time. This result was being read many different ways by the participants. Eventually, the judge was informed that the jury was deadlocked. He sent them back for more deliberations.

Finally, the judged was informed that the jury was hopelessly deadlocked. Four had determined that Carole Benson was guilty, while eight had determined that she was not guilty. The judge reluctantly determined that it was a hung jury and dismissed the jury. A polling of the jury confirmed that the result was four guilty and eight not guilty. Interestingly, all seven men along with one woman found Carole Benson not guilty.

The prosecution team met with Detectives O'Brien and Harrington to discuss the results. The prosecution team showed their anger.

"She's as guilty as hell," said Les Carpenter, the lead prosecutor. "We will try this case again. That bitch can't get away with murder."

"She was good," chimed in Harrington. "She seduced the jury. At least the men on the jury. She had all the tools and she knew how to use all of them."

"Well, I need some time to think this through," added Carpenter. "But thinking about it right now, we are going to have another trial. She's as guilty as hell," he repeated himself.

Chapter Twenty-Three
Change in Plans

D etectives O'Brien and Harrington went to the office the next day to look over their open case files. As they sat at their desks reviewing various files, they couldn't refrain from talking about the case against Carole Benson.

"I was really surprised that she testified," said O'Brien.

"Same here," agreed Harrington.

"Did you notice that her testimony about being involved with Matt Simmons was almost the same as when we questioned her about a relationship with David Wilson," pondered O'Brien.

"Yea. Same script," concurred Harrington.

"Well, as was said before, good looks, great figure, she had all the tools. And she knew how to use them all," summarized O'Brien.

A short time later, their supervisor entered the office area, and announced, "I have some bad news for you, detectives."

O'Brien and Harrington must have been thinking—bad news! We know about the hung jury.

"What's the story?" O'Brien asked.

The supervisor looked at them and said, "I just got a call from the jail. Matt Simmons was found dead in his jail cell."

"What?" The detectives responded in unison.

"He apparently hanged himself last night," explained the supervisor.

"In his own mind, everything went wrong for him," said Harrington.

"But he got a good plea deal," said O'Brien.

"True," said Harrington, "but he lost what he thought was his lover. And he must have been thinking that he was going to spend time in prison while his so called lover would be entertaining other men."

"I don't know what to say," responded O'Brien. "You know she never came to see him after he was arrested. I'm sure he had a complete feeling of total abandonment and betrayal."

"I know what you're saying," concurred Harrington. "You're right on target with that, governor."

"Well, retirement might be what I should be thinking about now. I think I've had enough of this."

Before the end of the day, a call came in from the lead prosecutor. They would not pursue another trial. They lost their key witness. And they weren't about to take another loss.

David Wilson got word of the trial results and the death of Matt Simmons. He had little to say about anything. One thing was for certain.. He would now take the advice of his attorney. There would be no contact or communication of any kind with Carole Benson.

Detective Patrick O'Brien did in fact retire the following month. Detective Steve Harrington stayed on the force in his part time role with the police department. The two partnering detectives did occasionally get together at the local pub for a pint. There was always a lot to discuss between the Irishman and the Englishman.

Carole Benson continued to run her business, Premier Equipment, which continued to be successful.

Official records showed that the homicide of Charles Benson was concluded. There was a signed confession from the killer. The case was closed in the City of Baytown Beach in Orange County, California.

About the Author

After graduating from Northwestern University's School of Business, Frederick Bruce became a business counselor to small businesses. Clients ranged in size from one to ten people. Bruce later pursued a law career. He is currently a practicing attorney.

While engaged in these careers, Bruce encountered many interesting people and situations. As operators of small businesses, these clients often felt isolated and found Bruce to be one that they could confide in regarding business and personal matters. They felt comfortable and confident in his opinions and guidance. For Bruce, it often presented him with interesting and eye opening situations.

This is the third book written by Frederick Bruce, and his second murder mystery. His prior work was Murder at the Cathedral. His first book, The Blue Car, A Trilogy, tells the stories of three individuals seeking perfect lifetime careers. The stories are linked with a "pay it forward" symbolism.

Over the years , Bruce has worked with, and found the lives of people and their related stories very interesting . Although fictional, his experience has enabled him to share stories about people.

Lightning Source UK Ltd.
Milton Keynes UK
UKHW040216291022
411262UK00002B/488